"Nothing happens i[...] Poseidon said. **"Exc**[...] **sponsoring your service.**

"And if I say yes?"

"Then we'll get married, you enjoy lots of money and the warm approval of my very Greek grandmother, and her share of the trust will remain in family hands, as it should be."

Are you really going to go through with it?

Probably not, but again, she had to consider it. "I'll think about it," she said finally.

He had the grace to not look too satisfied. "Excellent." After reaching into his pocket, he pulled out a plain white card and held it out. "Here is the number to my private cell phone. I'd like an answer in a week, if possible, though if you need more time, let me know."

Andie reached for it, startled as her fingers brushed his and a ripple of electricity crackled through her. It nearly made her drop the card and she was surprised enough to look into his blue gaze to see if he felt it too.

A mistake.

Because she could see it, glowing in the blue depths of his eyes. Attraction. Interest. Chemistry.

The Teras Wedding Challenge

Twin brothers. One marriage challenge.
Will they win their unlikely brides?

When the powerful Greek Teras brothers are dared by their beloved grandmother to swap their playboy lifestyles for married life, they don't shy away. But when their unconventional brides are revealed, claiming them will prove harder than either could have imagined...

Asterion Teras's bride? Brita Martis, a rebellious woman seeking refuge in the local nunnery! Enjoy their passionate awakening in

A Tycoon Too Wild to Wed by Caitlin Crews

Poseidon Teras's bride? Andromeda Lane, the vivacious woman protesting outside his billion-dollar offices! Their combustible chemistry is unleashed in

Enemies at the Greek Altar by Jackie Ashenden

Both available now!

Enemies at the Greek Altar

JACKIE ASHENDEN

HARLEQUIN

PRESENTS

HARLEQUIN®
PRESENTS™

Recycling programs for this product may not exist in your area.

ISBN-13: 978-1-335-59346-7

Enemies at the Greek Altar

Copyright © 2024 by Jackie Ashenden

For questions and comments about the quality of this book, please contact us at CustomerService@Harlequin.com.

TM and ® are trademarks of Harlequin Enterprises ULC.

Harlequin Enterprises ULC
22 Adelaide St. West, 41st Floor
Toronto, Ontario M5H 4E3, Canada
www.Harlequin.com

Printed in Lithuania

MIX
Paper | Supporting responsible forestry
FSC® C021394

Jackie Ashenden writes dark, emotional stories with alpha heroes who've just gotten the world to their liking only to have it blown apart by their kick-ass heroines. She lives in Auckland, New Zealand, with her husband, the inimitable Dr. Jax, two kids and two rats. When she's not torturing alpha males and their gutsy heroines, she can be found drinking chocolate martinis, reading anything she can lay her hands on, wasting time on social media or being forced to go mountain biking with her husband. To keep up-to-date with Jackie's new releases and other news, sign up to her newsletter at jackieashenden.com.

Books by Jackie Ashenden

Harlequin Presents

The Innocent's One-Night Proposal
The Maid the Greek Married
His Innocent Unwrapped in Iceland
A Vow to Redeem the Greek

Rival Billionaire Tycoons

A Diamond for My Forbidden Bride
Stolen for My Spanish Scandal

Three Ruthless Kings

Wed for Their Royal Heir
Her Vow to Be His Desert Queen
Pregnant with Her Royal Boss's Baby

Visit the Author Profile page
at Harlequin.com for more titles.

To the wonderful Caitlin Crews, whose writing and heroes I have loved since before I was even published. Writing this duet with you has been the best.

CHAPTER ONE

'SO MUCH NOISE,' Dimitra Teras complained, peering out of the window of her grandson's London office. 'What is happening out there?'

Her grandson, Poseidon Teras, one half of the mighty Teras twins, lounged in his black leather chair, at his fastidiously clean and tidy desk, and regarded his grandmother with some amusement. 'Protestors, Yia Yia. Nothing exciting.'

Loud chants floated up from the square outside his office. Someone sounded as if they were in possession of a megaphone.

The protestors had been there all week and, quite frankly, Poseidon was getting tired of them. For some reason the little group had targeted him and had decided to tell the world that he was the root of all evil. That he was a misogynist, a monster. That he chewed people up and spat them out, mistreated his employees and on and on. The usual, in other words.

He was not, of course, any of those things, and nor did he do any of the things they accused him of. He liked women—no, he *loved* women—and, while his lovers were many, he never took advantage of anyone, let alone chewing them up and spitting them out. And as for his company—well. People competed for the chance to be employed by him. Hydra Shipping, the shipping and supply-chain company that he'd inherited from his father, and built up over the course of fifteen years so it now spanned the globe, was a fair and safe workplace. He'd made sure that it was. Not because he cared all that much about people, but because his business was more productive when his employees were happy. And if that made him a monster, then so be it. He didn't care what the media said about him, and he didn't care about the protestors either.

They, on the hand, clearly cared very deeply about him, and he was of the opinion that if he bothered them so very much, then perhaps they should go and do something more constructive than standing outside his building and shouting at him.

'What are they protesting about?' Dimitra continued to frown out of the window at the group.

'Oh, me. I'm the devil incarnate, apparently.'

He wasn't worried. A group of protestors shouting about how terrible he was remained at the bottom of his list of things to be concerned about. Not that he had a list. He only cared about three things in this world: his twin brother Asterion, his grandmother, and Hydra Shipping.

Dimitra turned her sharp gaze on him. 'Don't think I haven't forgotten about you.'

Ah, yes, his grandmother's edict: that he and his

brother were to marry a woman of her choosing, on pain of her share of the Teras family trust being given to an outsider. A fate worse than death.

Asterion had managed to find himself a bride—an ex-nun with an interest in wildlife, much to Poseidon's amusement—and was blissfully in love. Love was something that Poseidon had managed to avoid so far and was planning on continuing to avoid for the rest of his life.

Still, his grandmother wanted grandchildren and he cared about her wishes. He wouldn't make Asterion's mistake and actually fall in love with the woman Dimitra chose for him, but the marriage and producing children wouldn't be a problem. After all, it wasn't as if that was difficult. What woman in the world would say no to him? No one had so far. It was true that was largely in the bedroom, but for the chance to wear his ring? He couldn't think of a woman who'd refuse—and that wasn't being arrogant, that was just fact. He was handsome, rich, and powerful, and he'd generally found that to be an irresistible combination.

'I know you haven't forgotten me,' he said mildly. 'I have been awaiting your choice with bated breath.'

Dimitra's gaze narrowed. 'Always so uncaring. As if nothing matters. You should have someone who cares.'

Poseidon had once cared. He'd cared very deeply. He'd loved his father, had cared about and wanted his approval, his mother's too, but then they'd both died, along with his grandfather, in a car accident when he was twelve.

After that, seeking to fill the void left by his parents'

death, he'd found himself a mentor, a friend of his father's, and—

But he didn't think about that. Not any more. Just as he didn't think about caring. Caring was a weakness and not one he'd ever saddle himself with again.

'And what martyr would that be?' he asked. 'Do you have someone in mind? A virgin sacrifice, perhaps?'

Dimitra snorted and glanced out of the window again. Then she smiled.

Poseidon did not like that smile.

'Her,' Dimitra said with some certainty, pointing at the group of protestors below. 'That woman right there.'

Poseidon was aware of a certain sinking feeling, but he got up all the same and strolled over to the window.

The group outside was really only a collection of four people. He hadn't taken much notice of them earlier in the week, getting his security team to move them and the signs they were clutching along, before they started to become a nuisance. But today they'd been much louder than usual, and it wasn't until he came to the window and looked out that he saw why.

One woman had chained herself to the statue in the square in front of his building and she appeared to be wearing… Well… Nothing but body paint and a pair of very brief knickers. Her red hair was loose and wild down her back, and across her admittedly very generous chest were written the words *Poseidon Teras go to hell!*

He frowned. '*That* woman? Surely you're mistaken.'

But Dimitra had a very self-satisfied look on her face.

'Yes, Poseidon. That woman. If you can get *her* to marry you, I might not even insist on grandchildren.'

There was a note of challenge in his grandmother's voice, something that Poseidon could never resist, because he was competitive by nature and loved to win. His father used to say it was due to the minute between Asterion's birth and his own, so Poseidon was forever trying to catch up. The casual way his father had said it, as if it wasn't possible for Poseidon to match his brother in any way, had once been a source of pain to him, but he didn't care nowadays. On the contrary, now it gave him something to aim for.

'You think I couldn't get her to marry me.' He didn't make it a question.

His grandmother gave him a measuring glance. 'Not if she thinks you're the devil incarnate. Which makes her perfect. If you can get her to agree and actually bring her to the altar, then I'll consider you fully rehabilitated.'

This whole marriage farce—he couldn't think of it as anything else—was supposed to be for their own good. At least that was what Dimitra had told him and Asterion a few months earlier when she'd delivered her ultimatum. Because she wanted them to be good men, not monsters, and apparently the answer to that was marriage.

Privately he thought the whole idea ridiculous, but Dimitra had been adamant and, since Asterion had agreed, Poseidon could hardly say no.

He gazed without pleasure at his grandmother's choice of bride for him. She'd been painted to look like a mermaid, with blue, green, and gold scales covering most of lower body. Shells had been painted over her breasts to mimic a bra, and the rest of her skin was blue. The design was quite skilful, but wholly inappropriate for a public place.

She'd raised that wretched megaphone and was shouting something else through it, and there was now a small crowd gathered around the statue, staring at her. That was probably due more to her state of undress rather than what she was saying, but perhaps that was the point. She wanted attention and she was doing anything to get it.

Poseidon had no problem with women who spoke their mind and had strong opinions. What he found so distasteful was intensity, and this woman had *intense* written all over her.

'Really, Yia Yia?' he said. 'I was hoping for more of a challenge than that.'

'She will say no to you,' Dimitra pronounced. 'She will not fall at your feet like all the rest.'

Another chant rose. The mermaid was looking up at the windows now, her megaphone pointed in his direction as if she could actually see him, though he knew she wouldn't be able to. Not when he was on the top floor.

He could see her, though, and he couldn't help but notice that her body paint did nothing to hide full curves, all rounded and luscious, and that her hair was a glorious red-gold, hanging down her back in tangled ringlets, shining like a pirate's treasure. He couldn't make out her face but he was aware of a certain…frisson that moved through him as she looked in his direction, shouting through her megaphone. He knew what a frisson was. A forerunner to attraction.

Intriguing. A good thing to be attracted to the woman Dimitra had chosen. It would certainly make things easier.

'She really does not like you,' Dimitra observed. 'Good. I would not want this to be too easy.'

Poseidon didn't want it to be too easy either. Because the honest truth was that he'd become a little…bored. Hydra Shipping was doing extremely well and he was making money hand over fist. He enjoyed the competitive relationship he had with his twin, which the media made out to be much more contentious than it actually was, and he certainly enjoyed all the women who came to his bed.

Things *were* easy and, yes, he was getting tired of easy.

Perhaps his grandmother knew what she was doing after all.

'She is very…loud,' he said.

'Passionate,' Dimitra corrected. 'Not afraid to speak her mind. I think I will like her.'

'Passionate' was one word for all the chanting that was floating up to his window. But now that his grandmother had said it, Poseidon couldn't help but imagine how all that fervour would translate in the bedroom…

The woman tossed her lovely hair over one shoulder, then lowered her megaphone and raised her hand, giving him a very obvious one-finger salute.

The frisson that had chased down his spine became a very definite pulse.

Poseidon smiled.

Yes. Perhaps Dimitra was right. She was perfect.

Andromeda Lane lowered her hand. She'd been certain that someone in the huge Hydra Shipping building towering above her had been watching. She'd felt it. And, though they were too far up and the windows were slightly tinted, she was sure it had been someone important. Perhaps even that stone-cold bastard himself, Poseidon Teras. In which case she hoped he'd enjoyed her heartfelt gesture of appreciation.

Poseidon and his equally filthy-rich brother Asterion had always been fixtures in the gossip columns, but it was Poseidon's latest behaviour that had done it.

Two weeks ago he'd been photographed in a nightclub with a couple of very young women, both of them clearly intoxicated and plastering themselves all over him, and it had reminded her so forcefully of Chrissy that bile had almost choked her.

'The Sea Monster', the media called him, because of his shipping company and all the virgins he ate, or something equally ridiculous. Which should have made him anathema to all sensible people, but it seemed to have the opposite effect. People *liked* him. They thought he was a charming reprobate.

Only Andromeda knew the truth, and so something had to be done.

She'd taken action in the form of Chrissy's Hope, a

drug and alcohol addiction service for women, which she'd set up a year ago and named after her older sister who'd died five years earlier. It had helped thousands of women, but it was expensive to run and it always needed money, so she spent a lot of time campaigning, trying to raise its profile in order to get more sponsors.

After seeing that photograph of Poseidon with those two women, she'd decided that she was going to use him and his notorious reputation as a way to get eyes on Chrissy's Hope.

So she'd gathered her usual coterie of friends, Tom, Ayesha, and Jo, and had organised a protest outside the Hydra Shipping offices. Yet they'd been there a week and the lack of media attention was beginning to get frustrating.

Jo was handling all the social media platforms, while Tom managed the video. Ayesha had done the signs and then—after Andie had finally got sick of the lack of movement and decided to do something a little more eye-catching—she'd got out her body paints and given Andie a mermaid paint job.

A mermaid, since Hydra Shipping was all about the sea. But Andie wouldn't be a mute Ariel. She would be a mermaid who had a voice and wasn't afraid to use it.

Hydra Shipping security guards had moved their group on a couple of times, and Tom had been at the ready with his phone, waiting to film some brutality. But while the security people had been very firm, they'd also been gentle, and sadly brutality had been thin on the ground.

Andie had been annoyed. Not that she actually wanted violence, of course, but it would have helped the cause if Poseidon Teras's security team had been more…firm, or at the very least quite rude.

They hadn't been, though, and so she'd had to settle for being half-naked in mermaid body paint in order to get some attention.

There were a few people gathered around the statue, watching her, but most seemed uninterested, which was even more infuriating. They didn't know what men like Poseidon were really like. They were predators, preying on the weak and the vulnerable. People like her older sister.

Ayesha was handing out Chrissy's Hope pamphlets and Andie couldn't help but notice that most of the bystanders had either shaken their heads as Ayesha had approached, or surreptitiously chucked the pamphlets in a nearby bin.

It was enraging. Did they think they could just ignore the issue? That the terrible situations addiction and poverty got people into would just go away? That men like Poseidon Teras would stop taking advantage?

That was never going to happen, and she wasn't going to stop speaking out until people finally listened.

'Hey, Andie,' Tom called, pointing towards the front doors of the Hydra building. 'Something's happening.'

Andie lowered her megaphone and looked, because something was indeed happening. Security guards milled around in a little huddle, then abruptly the doors opened and a man strode through them.

He was very tall, with short, inky black hair, and a face that would have shamed the angels. His chest and shoulders would have done a gladiator proud, and he moved as if he owned every inch of the ground he walked on. Confident, arrogant, and known throughout the globe for his ruthless business practices, Poseidon Teras was the very epitome of the rich, powerful billionaire—and Andie loathed him and everything he stood for.

She didn't think as he approached. Didn't pause to consider whether shouting at the very famous CEO of a powerful company was a good idea. Fury burned in her blood. Because it had been this man's yacht and the party onboard it where Chrissy had died, and Andie held him personally responsible.

If she hadn't abhorred violence she would have punched him straight in his beautiful face, but since that wasn't an option, she decided to shout at him instead.

She lifted both her chin and her megaphone and yelled a variety of expletives detailing his parentage, his general demeanour, his apparent disregard for women, and his blatant male privilege, all in very rude, bordering on obscene detail.

If he found this offensive, he didn't show it, coming to a stop before the statue she'd chained herself to and giving her a steady, half-amused look while she continued to shout. Then, when she paused for breath, he asked in a deep, velvety voice, 'Have you finished?'

'No,' Andie snapped, because she hadn't. She had five years of rage simmering inside her. Now she'd caught his attention and he'd finally come down from his ivory tower, this was too good an opportunity to miss.

Are you sure you want his attention? You're naked and he's a known man-whore.

Andie wasn't averse to using her body to get eyes on a cause, nor did she care that a cotton G-string and a thin layer of body paint were the only things separating her from total nakedness. At least she'd never cared before. Yet now, the thought of being virtually naked in front of Poseidon Teras made an odd heat go through her. Which only added to her fury.

'Do go on, by all means.' Poseidon put his hands in the pockets of his dark grey suit trousers. 'I'm all ears.'

His eyes were the most incredible blue, indigo with shades of translucent green. Like the Mediterranean itself.

Much to Andie's rage, she found that not only had she caught her breath, she was also blushing. Incensed by this feminine betrayal, she lifted her megaphone again and prepared to give him another blast.

Poseidon took one hand out of his pocket and lifted a finger. 'But before you do,' he went on in the same level tone, 'I wonder if you wouldn't be more comfortable coming up to my office. Rain is forecast and I wouldn't want your body paint to get ruined.'

For a second Andie didn't know what to say. She hadn't expected him to actually come out of his building, let alone politely request her presence in his office.

What did I tell you? He also noticed the body paint.

Another small yet unmistakable pulse of heat went

through her. Infuriating. She didn't care if he looked at her body—and actually it was a good job if he did. Getting attention was the whole point.

The statue she'd chained herself to was on a plinth that gave her a bit of height, and she used it shamelessly, looking down at him with as much disdain as she could muster.

'Your office?' she asked. 'Why on earth would I want to come up to your office?'

'Because you clearly have a few things to say,' he said, as if it were obvious. 'I'll get my secretary to bring us some tea and we can have a civilised conversation that perhaps doesn't involve a megaphone.'

Andie opened her mouth to tell him that she was quite happy with the megaphone, but then Poseidon lifted another finger and abruptly a flood of security people began milling around her. One of them had some bolt cutters, which he used to cut the chain around her and the statue, while another somehow managed to nick her megaphone. Yet more were talking to Tom, Jo, and Ayesha, and leading them away.

'I don't want to come up to your office,' Andie said, pulling away from the security guard, who let her go without protest. 'And don't you dare touch me.'

'Wouldn't dream of it.' Poseidon was shrugging out of his suit jacket. 'But I'm sure you'd like some tea and your friends would like the lunch my security team is going to buy them.' He clicked his fingers. Another guard took the jacket from him and then, much to her shock, put it around her shoulders. It was still warm from his body and the dark charcoal wool smelled of some spicy scent, like amber or cedar. It was delicious, which was again enraging. She didn't want to like anything about him, including his scent.

She tried to shrug the jacket off, but soon found herself being hustled from the statue and ushered into the expensive hush of the Hydra Shipping offices.

Andie didn't mind sacrificing her pride for a cause, especially if it was for Chrissy's Hope. She debated fighting off his security and causing a scene in the lobby, since that would certainly get her attention.

Then again, he'd said he wanted to talk to her in his office and this could actually be a good thing. She could ask him about Chrissy, tell him about her and her death, and demand some justice. Financial restitution for Chrissy's Hope even. Because if they didn't find sponsorship soon, it was going to have to close.

So she said nothing, controlling her fury and letting the security guards escort her into the elevator and up to the top floor of the building. She stayed silent as they ushered her along an expensively carpeted hallway into a huge, plush office that was obviously Poseidon's.

There were big floor-to-ceiling windows along one wall that looked out over the square, and a huge wooden desk in pale wood that complemented the pale carpet. A large white leather couch plus several armchairs were arranged down one end, while sleek wooden shelves lined the wall opposite the windows.

Andie gazed around with some contempt. It was all very tasteful and reeked of money, which was as expected. She knew the Teras brothers, as everyone did—no one talked of anyone else, it seemed. Poseidon and his brother Asterion, who owned the Minotaur Group, were both of them darlings of the media.

Asterion had recently married, which had curtailed his exploits, but not so his twin. Poseidon was still as notorious as ever.

Well, she could use that. If he wanted a civilised conversation about why she was shouting outside his office, she'd tell him. She'd tell him everything. Hopefully that would shame him enough into giving her a huge donation or a sponsorship deal for Chrissy's Hope.

He hadn't come up in the elevator with her. She was just beginning to wonder if his promise of a chat had all been hot air when he entered the room, closing the door behind him and gesturing expansively to the white leather couch.

Andie didn't want to sit, since she was at a height disadvantage with him anyway, but the prospect of leaving body paint on the pristine white leather was too irresistible a chance to pass up. So she walked down to the other end of the office and sat down, keeping his jacket around her shoulders—because good luck with getting paint out of Italian merino.

Poseidon did not, as she'd expected, come to stand in front of her, looking down from his great height, intimidating her. Nor did he sit next to her on the couch, uncomfortably close. Instead, he pulled over a matching white leather armchair and sat down in it, all predatory grace, his blue gaze settling on her.

He was exquisitely dressed. His suit trousers looked handmade and tailored to fit his narrow waist and powerful thighs like a glove. He wore a black business shirt with a silk tie the same colour as his eyes. A heavy platinum watch circled one strong wrist.

She hadn't realised how unspeakably gorgeous and intensely charismatic his presence was in real life, and she hated how her mouth had gone dry in response. She hated that she was so shallow as to even notice his beauty.

She hated him, full stop.

'So,' he said, his deep voice warm, his blue gaze never dropping an inch from her face, despite the fact that all she wore was a pair of knickers, his jacket, and some blue, green, and gold paint. 'Care to tell me your name?'

It wasn't the first question she'd expected him to ask. Despite telling her he wanted a 'civilised conversation', she'd expected him to demand to know what she was doing and to cease disrupting his place of business, all while ogling her naked body. She'd even expected the police to be called, or at least some kind of threat to be issued, not a simple, 'Care to tell me your name?'

Andie folded her hands in her lap and lifted her chin. 'Guess.'

He smiled and the world just about slowed down and stopped. His mouth was just as beautiful as the rest of him, and his smile made it feel like summer.

Don't forget Chrissy. Don't forget what happened to her.

Oh, she would never forget. Their mother had been a single parent, working two jobs just to keep their heads above water. She hadn't noticed how bored seventeen-year-old Chrissy was, and how she'd wanted something more for herself, something better. Andie, too busy trying hard at school, hadn't noticed either—not then. It had only been when Chrissy had started going to nightclubs and had met Simon, the man who'd introduced her into the wrong crowd, that Andie had started to pay attention. And when Chrissy had started escorting, at Simon's suggestion, to pay for the lifestyle she'd developed a taste for, Andie had told their mother, who'd done precisely nothing.

'Why should I?' Chrissy had asked Andie, when Andie had begged her to stop escorting at least. 'It's fun and the money's good. I mean, really, Andie, do you want to be a waitress all your life?'

Her beautiful, intelligent, perfect, reckless sister. She'd got caught up in the world of the rich and famous, spirited away like a mortal into the faerie realm. And she'd ended up dying of an overdose on Poseidon's yacht during a party.

He and Simon had destroyed her and, while Simon was long gone, Andie wasn't going to let Poseidon get away with it. Certainly the very last thing she'd *ever* do was fall for him herself. So she ignored his beautiful smile and the way it made her heart beat fast, and stared at him as if he was dirt underneath her shoe instead.

Sadly this seemed to have no effect.

'You don't like me,' he said sympathetically. 'I understand. But if you don't tell me your name, I'll have to call you something like "little siren". Since you are little and have been singing a very loud song all week.'

The soft roughness of his lightly accented voice, not to mention the dry amusement in his tone, slid under Andie's skin like a burr, making her bristle.

'While you,' she said, 'are the most privileged, arrogant, misogynistic bastard I have ever had the misfortune to meet.'

His smile deepened as if she'd said something funny. 'Two of those things are absolutely true, and two are not. I am certainly privileged and arrogant, but I assure you that my parents were married. Also, I don't hate women. On the contrary, I am an ardent feminist.'

He was making fun of her, wasn't he?

'I'm glad you find taking advantage of women so amusing,' she said hotly. 'Because I don't.'

His gaze narrowed. 'Excuse me? I don't take advantage of anyone, little siren, let alone women.'

'Then how do you explain that nightclub picture?'

She hadn't meant to reveal her hand quite so quickly. Then again, why not? She was always honest about her concerns at least.

He frowned. 'What nightclub picture?'

'The one from last week.' How dared he not remember? 'With the two women who were obviously very young and highly intoxicated.'

The frown cleared. 'Oh, that. They were at the bar and causing a fuss because the barman discovered they were underage. I waited with them to make sure they didn't get themselves into trouble, while a taxi was called to take them home.'

He said it so casually that she was half inclined to believe him, though very much against her will.

'That is not what the papers said,' she snapped.

'No, because that doesn't make for good copy, does it?' He gave her a shrewd glance. 'What? Did you think I was there to debauch underage girls?'

Andie's face felt hot but she refused to look away. 'Well, were you?'

He didn't answer immediately, continuing to give her a steady, assessing look that made her feel as if he was stripping a layer of skin away.

'You're very angry with me, aren't you?' he observed at last. 'It can't be only about those pictures. Tell me, what did I do?'

Andie was always honest and so she gave him the truth. 'You're responsible for the death of my sister, and what I want to know is what you're going to do about it.'

CHAPTER TWO

SITTING OPPOSITE THE little siren, Poseidon rapidly became aware of two things. First, it was *not* going to be as easy to get her to marry him as he'd thought. Second, Dimitra was wrong. She was *not* perfect. Not at all. And he'd known that the moment he'd come out of his building to confront her.

She'd stood on her plinth, looking down at him with furious contempt. Shouting at him through her megaphone and calling him all the names under the sun. He'd never had anyone shout at him like that before— he was a powerful man; no one would dare—and he'd been…shaken. Because she was magnificent. There was simply no other word for her. Proud in her nakedness, with his name written boldly across the curves of her full breasts, staring at him with eyes the most beautiful shade of green he'd ever seen. Light and clear, like sunshine on fresh new leaves.

There had been fire in her, and intensity, and the frisson he'd felt up in his office had turned into a kick of heat so strong it had taken him by surprise.

He hadn't liked it. He hadn't liked it at all. Any feeling with the power to grip him by the throat like that was suspect, and that included physical desire.

Sex he indulged in whenever he felt like it, and with anyone he wanted who also wanted him. He never had to work for it. He never *wanted* to work for it. But this woman had *work* written all over her—which made her instantly off-limits to him. The strength of his physical attraction also made her off-limits.

He never wanted to desire someone so badly he lost all sense. Desire was manageable, controllable, and so he controlled it ruthlessly.

But he'd also known pretty much straight away that this woman was *not* going to mindlessly accept a marriage proposal from him.

Dimitra had wanted both him and Asterion to court the women she'd chosen for them and then to marry them, as proof they weren't complete monsters. Asterion had once been dubbed the Monster of the Mediterranean, and he was certainly a monster no longer—not now his Brita had tamed him.

Poseidon had no intention of being tamed, and nor did he want to change his already very comfortable life. He liked things the way they were, and he certainly wasn't going to alter his behaviour just because he had a wife.

So while Dimitra might have insisted on a courtship, as he'd ushered the little siren up to his office he'd had a better idea—one that gave him more certainty and might make her more open to at least listening to him.

Except then she'd sat on the couch in his office, draped in the jacket he'd given her, partly for her own modesty and partly because he'd had to cover at least some of those luscious curves, and he'd found himself... transfixed.

Go to hell Poseidon Teras was staring him in the face, sparks of anger in her green eyes, her chin jutting. And the uncompromising and blunt way she spoke, looking at him as if he was nothing more than dirt beneath her shoe...

All of her was fascinating and he'd let himself become distracted.

His lovers were all women who were as jaded as he was...as bored and as cynical. They never required anything of him but pleasure, so that was what he gave them. He could make them come, but whether they liked him or otherwise he didn't know and didn't care.

But not this woman. She was actively furious with him and now he knew why. However, while he was a certified playboy, who'd spent many nights with many women and sometimes more than one, he'd never been directly involved with anyone's death before.

He frowned. 'Your sister? Please explain.'

'You own a yacht called *Thetis*,' she said, in her light, clear voice. 'And you often use it for parties.'

He did have a yacht called *Thetis*—it was one of many he owned—and he sometimes used it for parties. 'Yes,' he said slowly. 'That is correct.'

'Five years ago there was a party on board the *Thetis* and a woman died.'

The siren's green eyes glittered with anger and a few other deep, passionate emotions he didn't recognise.

'That woman was my sister.'

A pulse of shock went through him. There had been an incident, he recalled now, when he'd loaned *Thetis* to an acquaintance, who'd then had a different friend organise a party on board. Poseidon hadn't been involved with the organisation, though he'd briefly considered attending. He'd decided not to in the end, because he'd had an upcoming business trip. It hadn't been until he'd returned to London that he'd been notified about the death of a woman at that party. An investigation had been conducted, which he'd fully co-operated with, and in the end the organiser of the party had been prosecuted. He'd sent some money to the woman's family to help with funeral expenses, and he'd never loaned out his yachts to anyone ever again.

He hadn't thought of the incident since.

Now, it was clear why the woman sitting opposite him, straight-backed and defiant, her gaze unwavering, was so full of righteous anger towards him.

'I'm so very sorry,' he said, and meant it, because he knew what it was to lose people you loved. 'I hope you received the money I sent for her funeral.'

The siren's pointed chin lifted higher, the green sparks in her gaze becoming flames. 'Money. That's all you care about,' she spat. 'As if that could make up for losing Chrissy.'

Grief—that was the other emotion in her eyes. It was grief.

He knew about grief. He knew how it could hollow you out and turn you into a shell. How it could make you desperate, a target for anyone to manipulate. Well, she was safe from him in that respect at least. He'd had his own grief for his parents used against him and he wouldn't wish that on anyone else.

So he was going to need to be careful, since he had no desire to make it worse for her. But she did have to know that he had nothing to do with her sister's death.

'As I said, I'm very sorry for the loss of your sister,' he said gently. 'But I was not on the boat at the time, nor did I have anything to do with that party.'

This didn't seem to mollify her, because her expression didn't change. She still looked furious. 'Whether you were on it or not, you owned the boat and it was your responsibility.'

Clearly she was looking for someone to blame, which was fair. And he supposed his response might have sounded a little like an excuse. He couldn't remember exactly what the organiser of that party had received in the way of justice, but it had been a jail term. Though, of course, as she'd said, none of that would bring her sister back.

He gave her an assessing glance. 'What would you like me to do in that case?'

There was an uncompromising slant to her jaw, and she answered without the slightest hesitation. 'You can sponsor the drug and alcohol addiction service I've named after my sister. For the next five years.'

Poseidon was aware of deep surprise, since he'd been expecting a demand for personal recompense, which was what most people wanted in these situations. He hadn't expected a sponsorship request for a charitable service.

'*You* don't want money?' he clarified, just to be sure.

'*I* don't need money.' She gave him a look as if he'd personally offended her. 'But Chrissy's Hope does.'

He was still surprised, but it did seem a reasonable request. He had more money than he knew what to do with, quite honestly, and he could spare it. But he also wasn't a master of business for nothing, and here was an opportunity. A way for them to both get what they wanted.

You weren't going to use her anger and grief against her, remember?

And he wouldn't. This was a…business proposition, that was all. He required her to marry him and she needed money for her service. All he needed was her presence at the altar, an appearance of willingness enough to satisfy Dimitra, and her signature on their marriage certificate. He didn't need to sleep with her or, indeed, anything else. And in return he'd offer to sponsor her service for as long as she needed. Easy.

She was sitting up very straight on his couch, not making even one attempt to cover herself, her opinion of him written loud and clear on her skin. Her gaze was very direct and almost searing in its honesty, and he felt that heat kick inside him again. She had the delicate, pale skin of a redhead beneath all the paint, and he found himself wishing he had a damp cloth so he could wipe the paint away, discover the texture of her skin and the shape of her beneath it.

But no, he wasn't going to give in to that heat, not with her, and certainly not now he knew about her sister. He didn't care about people's feelings as a rule, because once you cared that was a slippery slope. You could be manipulated...you could be used. Feelings were a vulnerability, a weakness, and caring was a chink in your armour.

The easiest answer was simply not to care and so he didn't. However, he had his own personal lines that he would not cross. He did not manipulate people and he did not take advantage of them. Not in business and not in anything else. That didn't mean he wasn't ruthless—he was just honest about it.

He could flirt with this siren. He could probably bring her around to his way of thinking at some point, using either his charm or his looks to get her to give him what he wanted. But she was furious and grieving, and to do that would be wrong.

He would, however, use her need for money to his advantage. He had no qualms at all about that.

'Well?' she said when he didn't speak.

So it seemed that not only did she have a temper, she was impatient too. She had her hands folded in her lap and one finger was tapping the back of her other hand. The rest of her was very still, but it felt forced. As if she was containing herself, directing all that passion and fire into the blaze of her green eyes.

Pull yourself together and stop staring at her.

Annoyed with himself, Poseidon ignored the pull of his fascination and leaned forward, elbows on his knees, hands clasped between them. 'Very well,' he said. 'I will sponsor your service. But only on one condition.'

Somehow she managed to look down her nose at him, though even sitting down he was taller than she was. 'Of course there's a condition. God forbid you actually donate money to a worthy cause.'

'I'm a businessman, little siren, and I don't much care about your opinion of me, or indeed anyone else's opinion of me. And I need something from you.'

He didn't miss how she tensed, and it was clear she was expecting him to ask her for something distasteful, and, given her view of him, no doubt she was expecting it to be sexual.

'Naturally,' she said. 'Men like you never do anything for free, do you?'

'I don't know about other men like me, but no, I don't,' he agreed. 'And certainly in this instance I don't.'

'I suppose your condition is that I have to sleep with you.' She somehow made the statement defiant, challenging, and contemptuous all at the same time. 'In which case the answer is no, and if you dare touch me I'll call the police.'

His fascination tugged at the leash he'd put on it. She was small, very naked, and in the presence of one of the most powerful men in Europe. Yet she acted as if she was encased in a full suit of armour, carrying a sword, and leading a whole army into battle.

She was either very brave or very foolish, and he couldn't decide which.

'What would you call the police with?' he asked,

momentarily diverted. 'You're clearly not carrying a phone—unless you're very clever at hiding it.'

She sniffed, as if he'd said something unbearably stupid. 'There's a phone on your desk.'

'True. But you'd have to go past me to get it.'

Her eyes narrowed. 'I know self-defence. I'd break your nose.'

That made him want to smile, because she was so very fierce. 'No doubt,' he murmured. 'Rest assured, though, you're safe from me. I don't touch women who don't want to be touched.'

She eyed him, doubt clear on her face, while he stared blandly back. 'Perhaps you should ask me what my condition is instead of assuming,' he suggested.

'Perhaps you should tell me instead of playing stupid games.'

Oh, she is delicious.

The heat inside him kicked harder, bringing with it a sensation he hadn't felt for years, almost like…anticipation. But no, he couldn't start thinking like that. What he was proposing was a business deal, nothing more.

'Fine,' he said. 'I'll sponsor your service indefinitely. On the condition that you marry me.'

At first Andie didn't quite understand, because what he'd said didn't make any sense. 'Marry you?' she said blankly. 'Why?'

Poseidon was sitting forward with his hands clasped loosely between his knees, an almost apologetic look on his beautiful face. She was sure that wasn't real—that he wasn't actually apologetic. In fact, she was positive most things about him weren't real, including the fact that he *wasn't* responsible for Chrissy's death.

He *had* sent money for her funeral, along with an apology. She remembered that. But Miranda, Andie's mother, hadn't given Andie any details of the apology or the amount of money he'd given her. And Andie hadn't asked. The pair of them had been too mired in grief at the loss of their perfect, beautiful daughter and sister, crushed by the hole in their lives Chrissy's loss had left.

She'd died on this man's yacht and, despite what he'd said about not being responsible, the fact remained that if he hadn't loaned the yacht to a friend, there wouldn't even have been a party for Chrissy to go to.

And of course there would be a condition in return for his sponsorship of Chrissy's Hope. He wouldn't do it out of the goodness of his heart—that kind of man never did. He probably didn't even have a heart. He was, as he'd said, a businessman, and Andie knew all about businessmen. Simon had been a businessman, and so had all his friends. Chrissy had told her many stories about them when she'd started escorting—about their arrogance, their money, and their privilege. Chrissy had found them exciting. Certainly more exciting than the boys at school or on the council estate where they'd both grown up.

And Andie had agreed.

It hadn't been until after Chrissy had died that the truth had come out.

They weren't exciting. They were predators. And

Poseidon Teras was one of them—which meant she needed to be on her guard around him.

Now, he gave a theatrical sigh and said, 'Why? Because my grandmother is an old dragon and has decided, in her wisdom, that my brother and I should marry women of her choosing. And, sadly for you and I, your little performance with the megaphone attracted her attention, and she decided that the woman for me would apparently be you.'

Despite her best intentions, she felt the shock return, and for a moment it even made her forget her anger. 'Me?' she squeaked. 'Why me?'

'I think she was taken with your varied curses,' Poseidon said. 'I've been called many things in my time, but I have to admit you put them all together in a very creative way.'

Andie stared at him, nonplussed. 'I still don't understand.'

He lifted one powerful shoulder. 'The ways of my grandmother are varied and mysterious. Who can say why you? Possibly because you don't like me and were vocal about it.'

'She chose me because I don't like you?'

'Yes.' Poseidon smiled that devastating smile again. 'She likes a game.'

Andie struggled to hide her shock, because she really didn't want him to know how badly he'd surprised her. Anger was her go-to, her fuel, her engine. Anger was easy and familiar. While shock felt like…helplessness. Like standing in the hallway of the council flat where she'd lived with her mother, listening to a policeman tell her that her beloved older sister had died.

She went for anger now. 'You can't possibly think I'm going to agree,' she said hotly. 'What a stupid idea.'

'I heartily concur,' he replied, much to her annoyance. 'It is a stupid idea. But my grandmother is very insistent.'

Marry him. Marry Poseidon Teras—the man who wasn't quite as responsible for her sister's death as she'd thought, but who'd still had a hand in it. A man who was the epitome of everything she'd spent years fighting against.

It was impossible. Insanity.

A sudden suspicion gripped her. 'Is this some kind of elaborate joke? Because if so, I'm not—'

'It's not a joke, believe me.' His smile had become a little sharp, like a shark's, and it came to her suddenly that perhaps he didn't like the idea any more than she did.

'You don't actually want to marry me, do you?' she asked.

'I don't want to marry anyone, but what can you do?' He opened his hands. 'Dimitra is a force of nature and will not be denied.'

'That's ridiculous.'

'You've never met a Greek grandmother, I see.'

'So, what? You do everything she says?'

'No, but in this instance, if we don't marry, she's made it clear that her share of the family trust will go to someone who isn't family.' Again, he looked apologetic. 'It's important to my brother and I that her share does not go to outside hands.'

He said it so reasonably, Andie almost found herself nodding in agreement.

'Don't worry,' he continued. 'I won't be requiring sex, if that's what you're worried about. It'll be a paper marriage to fulfil her wishes, nothing more.'

At the word 'sex' a little spark of heat streaked through Andie, making her aware once more of her nakedness, of how his blue gaze hadn't dipped once to look at her body, and she found herself wondering why. Because when she used it as a weapon of protest it certainly got her attention, and usually from men.

Poseidon Teras was a well-known womaniser, so why wasn't he ogling her as she'd expected him to? Why hadn't he made a pass at her or even dropped a double entendre? Surely he'd be the first man to insist on sex along with this ridiculous marriage proposal.

'No sex?' she said, before she could think better of it. 'So you're going to stay celibate?'

'I did not say that.'

For a moment something glittered in those blue eyes…something hot and wicked. And the spark inside Andie ignited into a small flame, her brain taking the image of Poseidon Teras not staying celibate and running with it. He'd had a lot of lovers—the media was constantly full of pictures of him and his latest conquests, all of them as beautiful as he was. In the course of reading about him before the protest, she'd discovered he was reputed to be an excellent and generous lover, with all his exes going into raptures about his bedroom skills. And now she couldn't help but picture exactly what those skills were and what they would feel like…

No. What was she thinking? She'd specifically avoided men and their complications after what had happened to Chrissy, and she'd certainly never met anyone since then who'd made her change her mind.

This man would definitely *not* be the first—especially if his attitude to marriage was 'pay someone to marry me'.

'You wouldn't be faithful?' she asked. 'At all?'

He tilted his head slightly to the side, that faintly wicked gleam in his eyes becoming more pronounced. 'Why? Would you like me to be?'

Her cheeks warmed, which was irritating, but she didn't look away. A part of her wanted to, but it would feel too much as if she was giving ground. 'No,' she said. 'I don't care what you do. Except you mentioned sponsoring Chrissy's Hope indefinitely, right?'

'Yes,' he said. 'That's correct.'

You can't be seriously considering this.

She wasn't. Not at all. It was completely out of the question, not to mention insane. Then again, Chrissy's Hope was very important, and if there was even a chance it could be sponsored indefinitely she had to at least explore the offer. Even if he wasn't serious about it.

'And this would be regardless of how long we stay married?'

'Yes,' he repeated. 'Irrespective of a later divorce,

Hydra Shipping will commit to the deal until you decide to end it.'

It would mean she'd never have to go scraping around for funds again. All those desperate people who needed help would be given it, and she'd never have to turn anyone away.

It had been such a struggle, keeping the service going, and demand was increasing by the day. It needed money—a lot of money—in order to operate even the most basic services, let alone provide the support she wanted it to.

'How much are you offering?' she asked bluntly, and then told him how much it took to operate on a daily basis.

He didn't even blink. 'I'll double it.'

Andie's stomach dropped away. Double? God, there were so many things she could do with that…so much she could offer. Perhaps widening the scope of the service so that it would provide support for general health as well as for addiction. Better facilities too…

She became conscious that she was staring at him and that her shock was probably obvious. That wouldn't do. He couldn't be allowed to see how desperate she was, because she certainly wasn't going to beg. She was owed this. *Chrissy* was owed this.

'Okay,' she said, keeping a fixed expression on her face. 'And all that for simply agreeing to marry you? Which would be…what? My name on a piece of paper?'

She wasn't precious about the institution of marriage itself. Chrissy had told her enough hair-raising stories about the men she'd gone out with, who'd cheated on their wives and girlfriends, to make Andie highly sceptical over it. Her mother had separated from Andie's father when Andie had been a baby, and she'd never had a good word to say about it either.

However, Andie wasn't naive enough to think it would be as simple as her name on a piece of paper. There had to be more to it than that.

Poseidon nodded. as if he was pleased with the question. 'It will be a legal marriage, with a ceremony. Dimitra does love a wedding. Also, you'll have to pretend as if you're madly in love with me, otherwise she'll start to get suspicious.'

Andie frowned. He hadn't mentioned *that*. She wasn't very good at pretending. She prided herself on her honesty, and she lived her truth every single day. Pretence was anathema to her.

'You want me to pretend I'm in love with you?' She had to ask, just to be clear.

Again, he gave her an almost apologetic look. 'A little, perhaps. Dimitra wanted Asterion and I to court our respective wives, not pay them to be with us, and she'll be very unhappy if she discovers that that is indeed what I've done. Also,' he went on, before she could respond, 'we'll have to have a honeymoon. I hope that won't be a problem?'

So a wedding ceremony, acting as if she was in love with him, and now a honeymoon? Was he mad?

'It's a problem,' she snapped.

He held up a hand. 'Don't worry, we'll have separate

rooms. And there will be no obligation for you to provide any...wifely duties, so to speak. The honeymoon will be entirely for show. You could even think of it as a well-earned holiday.'

A holiday? With him?

It certainly wasn't anything she'd want to do herself, that was true. But she couldn't ignore the sponsorship for Chrissy's Hope. There was so much good she could do with that money. Surely she had to consider it at least?

She gave him a narrow look. 'If I agree, I'm not living with you. And I'm not giving up any part of my life for you.'

'Of course not,' he said smoothly. 'I wouldn't ask you to. We can deal with the living arrangements later.'

'And I want the sponsorship deal in writing and all the paperwork done before any kind of wedding ceremony. I want the terms of the marriage agreement in writing too, and signed.'

He nodded. 'I can arrange that.'

Andie waited, expecting some kind of counter offer in return, but he remained silent. Which was suspicious. He'd agreed to everything so quickly and hadn't protested. Was she missing something?

'How long would we have to stay married?' she asked after a moment's thought.

'Legally? Until Dimitra passes away, I would think. But she's very old, so I'm sure that won't be too long.'

Andie did not like his casual tone one bit. 'That's a terrible way to talk about your grandmother,' she said.

His eyes widened at that and it hit her, very belatedly,

that he wasn't just some guy. He was Poseidon Teras, a powerful billionaire, and not only had she called him all the names under the sun earlier, and accused him of being complicit in Chrissy's death, she'd also just pulled him up sharp about his grandmother. As if she had a right to it.

Andie could apologise when she was wrong—she had no problem with that. But she didn't like apologising to men who didn't deserve it. And he didn't deserve it. So she only stared at him belligerently, despite her cheeks being hot yet again, daring him to call her on it.

But all he did was study her in a way that made her want to shift around on the couch. He wasn't leering and he wasn't ogling. He only looked at her as if she was… interesting to him.

Which hadn't been her intention.

She didn't want to attract his interest, only his attention.

'You're very forthright, aren't you?' he observed at last, almost sounding admiring.

Disconcerted, she shrugged it off. 'I call it like I see it.'

'Indeed you do.' Then, rather to her surprise, he smiled again, and this time it was warm and natural, and, quite frankly, even more devastating than his previous smiles. 'I like that.'

Another thing she didn't want. Him to like anything about her. Him to…surprise her. She hated it…just as she hated that beautiful smile of his.

'Good for you,' she said. 'But I don't care about your opinion.'

'Oh, I think you do,' he murmured. 'If you didn't, you wouldn't have spoken to me so sharply about Dimitra. And you're right, by the way, it *is* a terrible way to speak about her.'

For a second she couldn't think what to say to that, but he didn't give her a chance to think, because then he went on. 'So? What's it to be, little siren? Is it a no? Or would you like to think about it?'

She eyed him. 'What happens if I say no?'

'Nothing happens if you say no,' he said. 'Except I will not be sponsoring your service and, perhaps worse, you'll disappoint Dimitra.'

'And if I say yes?'

'Then we'll get married, you'll enjoy lots of money and the warm approval of my very Greek grandmother, and her share of the trust will remain in family hands— as it should be.'

Are you really going to go through with it?

Probably not. But, again, she had to consider it. The opportunity for Chrissy's Hope was too good to pass up.

'I'll think about it,' she said finally.

He had the grace not to look too satisfied. 'Excellent.' Reaching into his pocket, he pulled out a plain white card and held it out. 'Here is the number for my private cell phone. I'd like an answer in a week, if possible. Though if you need more time, let me know.'

Andie reached for it, startled as her fingers brushed his and a ripple of electricity crackled through her. It nearly made her drop the card, and she was surprised enough to look into his blue gaze to see if he felt it too.

A mistake.

Because she could see it, glowing in the blue depths of his eyes. Attraction. Interest. Chemistry.

She blushed like a rose and jerked her hand back before she knew what she was doing.

Now you've given yourself away.

Andie ignored the whisper in her head. It had been static, nothing else. Because she hated him. She certainly *wasn't* attracted to him—not on any level.

Deciding that she was done with being here in his presence, Andie slid off the couch. 'A week should be fine,' she said crisply, and then, without another word, she turned to the doors and headed towards them.

She was halfway across the room when she remembered his jacket was still around her shoulders. So she stopped and shrugged, allowing the jacket to slip onto the floor. Then she turned her head and glanced at him over her shoulder. 'Oh, and by the way, my name is Andromeda.'

Leaving him with that, she turned back to the doors again and went out.

CHAPTER THREE

THAT NIGHT POSEIDON had his promised dinner with Dimitra, since she was flying back the next morning to the Mediterranean island kingdom that was the Teras family seat, and was suitably vague when she questioned him about Andromeda. He didn't want to give anything away about his plans, but she was naturally suspicious, so he had to walk a fine line.

However, when he got back to his London residence—a penthouse near the Hydra Shipping office that gave a perfect view over the Thames—he called his brother to discuss it.

'Did you tell her she'll need to come to the island?' Asterion asked, after Poseidon had related what had happened with Andromeda.

He sounded vaguely disapproving, which annoyed Poseidon irrationally.

Then again, he was already annoyed by how his thoughts kept returning to the siren as she'd left his office. How her fingers had brushed his as she'd taken his card—it hadn't been intentional on either part, he was sure—and the pulse of electricity that had followed. It had been deep, strong, a gut-punch of attraction. But nothing he couldn't have handled if he hadn't seen the flare of response in her eyes.

She might not like him, and she might be furious with him, but she'd felt the pull of their chemistry as deeply as he had—he was certain.

That's not going to make things easier.

It would certainly make things more…challenging. A beautiful woman whom he wanted and who wanted him had always been a temptation he could never resist. But this was a business proposal, not an actual marriage, and he'd decided he wasn't going to touch her. So he wouldn't. It was as simple as that.

He'd also been clear about what he expected from their potential wedding agreement. Or, at least, mostly clear. He'd neglected to mention a couple of things, as Asterion had pointed out. Such as the wedding ceremony in the ancient church that Dimitra so loved. But, again, it might not be an issue.

The island kingdom was where the Teras family had lived for generations, and where the Minotaur Group, Asterion's half of the family holdings, and Hydra Shipping, his half, had had their start.

It was beautiful, the island, a jewel in the middle of the deep blue of the Mediterranean, just off the coast of Greece. Tourists flocked to it every year and he was sure Andromeda would love it.

Will she, though? She's clearly not enamoured of anything about you.

That didn't matter. He didn't need her to be enamoured of him. He only needed her to agree to be his wife, that was all.

'No,' he said to his brother. 'I haven't told her. She hasn't agreed to marry me yet.'

Asterion made another disapproving sound, and started in with one of his lectures about how paying for a bride wasn't what Dimitra had intended, and how taking shortcuts wasn't a good idea, but Poseidon tuned him out, as he always did when Asterion decided to instruct him on something. His brother sometimes acted as if he was a full ten years older than Poseidon rather than only a minute.

Mainly, though, he tuned out Asterion because his thoughts had once again turned to Andromeda. How she'd paused on her walk out of his office and shrugged, letting his jacket slip from her shoulders and fall to the floor. How she'd glanced at him over her shoulder, gloriously naked apart from that tiny pair of knickers and her body paint, her clear green eyes meeting his.

'My name is Andromeda,' she'd said grandly, as if giving him a gift.

And the curious thing was that it *had* felt like a gift.

Asterion kept talking, while Poseidon again went over the questions she'd asked him about the marriage proposal, and how she'd narrowed her gaze as she'd demanded everything in writing and signed.

She was an excellent businesswoman, he couldn't help thinking. But Asterion was right about one thing: Dimitra wouldn't like it if she found out his marriage was basically a business deal. The whole point was for him to 'woo' the woman Dimitra had chosen, not pay her to be his bride.

In which case, he needed to be seen to be 'wooing'. It wasn't something he was used to doing, since women came to him, not the other way around. Besides, he certainly knew how to get a woman screaming his name. But a) while Andromeda might want him, she certainly wasn't going to admit it to him, and b) he'd already decided he wasn't going to use sex to get what he wanted.

Which meant he was going to have to do things differently. Except how to court a woman he knew nothing about and make it look sincere? At least from the outside?

He couldn't use the obvious gifts—jewellery et cetera—because this woman who could have demanded anything from him in return for her name on the marriage certificate only wanted a donation for her addiction service. It seemed unlikely she'd be happy with, say, an expensive necklace or earrings, or a couture gown. It had to be something that would satisfy Dimitra's nosey tendencies too.

Aren't you jumping the gun? Andromeda hasn't even agreed to do it yet.

That was, alas, true. He'd given her a week to decide, and she could very well refuse, no matter what he offered her, which meant he had to do something that would ensure she didn't. Choice was important to him, but that didn't mean he couldn't influence things a little.

'This is not one of your games, Poseidon,' Asterion

growled in his ear, obviously coming to the end of his lecture. 'And you cannot treat it as such.'

With some effort, Poseidon dragged his thoughts back to the conversation at hand. 'Is that disapproval I hear, brother mine? Surely not.'

'You're supposed to *woo* her, not pay her to stand at the altar.'

'Dimitra won't find out that I've paid her,' he said calmly. 'And I've already told Andromeda that she'll have to act as though she's in love with me. She was fine with it.'

She had *not* been fine with it, of course, but Poseidon could offer her some assistance with that before the actual wedding. Perhaps some practice would be in order. She'd have to get used to him touching her, for example. An arm around her waist, her hand in his, standing close...

You might even have to kiss her.

A burst of unwelcome heat went through him at the thought of that lush mouth under his. Would her taste be tart and sharp like citrus? Or would it be sweet and sugary? It would be hot, that was certain, and her curves under his hands would feel like—

But no. He wasn't going to be doing anything more than giving a brief touch here and there, and maybe a kiss. He wouldn't let himself get carried away. If he was really so worked up that a prickly little siren could get him hard, then he should go and find another woman—someone warm and soft and willing, not spiky and angry. Then again, finding himself a woman now, after Dimitra had chosen Andromeda for him, would risk undermining the illusion of romance he was trying to build. Better to wait until after he'd done his duty.

'I'm sure Andromeda was fine with that,' Asterion said dryly. 'And I'm also sure it'll work out exactly as you expect.'

Poseidon decided to ignore the blatant scepticism in his twin's tone. 'I need to at least make it look like I'm courting her. But she's not the kind of woman who likes jewels, which means I have to do something else.'

There was a silence.

'Wait…' There was a suggestion of amusement in Asterion's deep voice. 'Are you asking me for seduction tips?'

'*Courting* tips,' Poseidon corrected. 'I have to look as if I'm madly in love, and, as you know, I have no experience of that nonsense.'

'Take her to bed,' Asterion said. 'Isn't that what you normally do?'

Another of those unwelcome bolts of heat went through him. All those pretty curves, that smooth skin and passion… She would be fire in his hands, but he could direct it. He could turn all that glory on him and—

'No,' Poseidon said, both to his own thoughts and yet again to his brother, conscious that he was sounding too emphatic about it. 'It's a business deal.'

Another silence fell.

'I see,' Asterion murmured, his tone very neutral. 'Well, if it's a business deal, then I take it you have her agreement? Because you know that as soon as you make any kind of move the media will be onto it.'

Poseidon stilled. 'No,' he said slowly, because Asterion had just given him a very good idea. 'She hasn't agreed...' he paused '...yet.'

'You have a plan.'

It wasn't a question.

'Oh, yes.' Poseidon smiled. 'I have a very good plan indeed.'

Andromeda stared around the rundown waiting room of Chrissy's Hope at the end of the day, a deep feeling of discomfort sitting inside her.

She'd tried to make the place look welcoming, but it was difficult when the only rooms she'd been able to afford for the service were situated in a shabby office block, and there was no money left over for anything resembling decor.

She'd put up a couple of nice pictures of scenery cut from some travel magazines, and there was a small vase of freesias on the rickety table, which she'd nicked from someone's garden. But the plastic chairs she'd rescued from the side of the road, so clients could have somewhere to sit, were scratched, the worn grey paint on the walls drained the pictures of life, and the freesias were drooping.

It was depressing. Hardly living up to the 'hope' in Chrissy's Hope.

Money. You need money. You need Poseidon Teras.

Andromeda scowled harder, then turned and went

back behind the second-hand reception desk she'd managed to source for free from a recycled furniture website.

She'd deliberately forgotten about Poseidon Teras for the past few days and she didn't want to remember him now.

You haven't forgotten. Not even deliberately.

She didn't want to admit it. She didn't want to admit that the man had been lurking in her brain, like the monster he was, ever since she'd walked out of his office. His astonishing blue eyes, and the electricity she'd felt when she'd brushed his hand, had seared themselves into her memory…a burn so deep that no amount of running mental cold water on it seemed to get rid of the heat.

Perhaps she hated him a little less than she had, knowing he wasn't ultimately responsible for Chrissy's death and that he'd paid for the funeral, but she still hated him and everything he stood for. And as for this marriage proposal… It was preposterous. How could she even think about taking it seriously?

Men like him never kept their word, and they never did what they promised. Simon, the man Chrissy had met in the VIP area of one of London's more exclusive nightclubs, had promised her the world, yet he'd given her drugs and led her to her doom. Men lied. All the time. And Poseidon was surely no different.

Except he agreed to all your demands, including that he put it all in writing.

True…he had.

Not forgetting his offer of sponsorship indefinitely, not dependent on the marriage…

Andromeda scowled harder. He was using Chrissy's Hope against her to get what he wanted. It was manipulation, pure and simple.

He's not manipulating you into anything but your name on a piece of paper and a bit of theatre. Calm down.

She rearranged the pens beside the pad on the desk, irritated, because that *was* actually true—as much as she hated to admit it. He was a businessman, he'd told her, and he didn't do anything for free. But...well, was what he'd done any different from what she would have done in his shoes? For Chrissy's Hope? He was doing it for his own selfish interests, while her motivations were more altruistic, but she'd have done anything if it meant saving her service. Including manipulating people.

Are your motivations really that altruistic? Aren't you doing this for you? Because you were silent when you should have spoken up? Because you let Chrissy die?

Andie shoved that thought from her head. She hadn't 'let' Chrissy die. And she *had* spoken up. It hadn't been her fault that their mother hadn't wanted to listen. Miranda had been thrilled for Chrissy, who had been mixing with 'the stars and all the famous people'. Chrissy was 'going places', Miranda had kept insisting, and Andie shouldn't complain about it because that looked like jealousy.

So Andie, fifteen and not knowing where else to turn, had stopped complaining and hoped that her sister would be fine.

Except she hadn't been fine.

It was too late for Chrissy now, but Andie was making up for what she hadn't done back then. All of this was for her sister's sake, not hers. It really was. To stop others from falling down the same addiction hole Chrissy had.

At that moment the waiting room door opened and a couple of men in black suits, with earpieces in their ears, came in. They both scanned the waiting room with professional eyes, then one held the door open, while the other stood at the ready beside it.

Andie stared at them in surprise, only to have the surprise turn to shock when Poseidon Teras strode through the open door.

Instantly a wave of heat washed over her, closely followed by an inevitable wave of anger. Because what on earth was *he* doing here? It hadn't been a week yet, and she still hadn't decided what she was going to do. He had no call to be coming into her place of business as if he owned it.

She shot to her feet, ready to demand the reason for his presence, when he stopped in front of the reception desk, his intense blue gaze fixed on her. With a flourish, he produced the biggest bunch of dark red roses she'd ever seen in her life.

'For you, my lady,' he said, in his deep, warm voice.

Andie blinked, shaken for a second. Flowers. He'd brought her flowers. No one had ever done that before. They were beautiful too, the velvety petals a deep red and with the most gorgeous scent.

'What are these for?' she asked, momentarily taken by surprise.

The beginnings of a smile curled his beautiful mouth. 'Because when a gentleman is courting a lady, he always brings her flowers. Also, I thought it might help your decision along.'

She found herself bristling, though she didn't quite know why. Perhaps because he'd surprised her and she didn't want to be surprised by him. She didn't want him to know he'd surprised her either.

Ignoring the flowers, she said, 'A week. You were going to give me a week to decide.'

'I am,' he agreed. 'I'm not here for an answer, Andromeda. I'm here to give you a token of my appreciation.'

She folded her arms, eyeing him, very conscious once again of how tall he was, how broad. How the force of his charisma was like a storm front blowing in, making everything inside her lift up and get whirled around in utter chaos.

He's like Simon, and you know it.

Simon, who'd led Chrissy down the path she'd followed with such abandon. He'd been rich, charismatic, and one night, after Chrissy had been dropped off home, Andie had peeked out through the curtains of her bedroom window and caught a glimpse of him. He'd been the most beautiful man Andie had ever seen. Chrissy had fallen for him and fallen hard, and that night Andie had fallen for him too. But she'd only been fifteen... a girl...while Chrissy had been twenty and a woman.

She hadn't been jealous—no matter what Miranda had said. She'd known she was too young and that

Chrissy was more beautiful, more fascinating than she'd ever be. But she'd been envious. Simon had taken Chrissy into his world of high-society parties, of beautiful gowns and champagne and trips to Monte Carlo, to Paris, to Cannes. And Andie hadn't been able to help wanting that too. To be taken away from the stifling confines of the council flat and the drudgery of school, and her part-time job in the supermarket. Swept off her feet by a handsome man and taken into a bigger, more exciting life.

Until it had all gone to hell.

Poseidon Teras was that kind of hell. He was even richer and more charismatic and more beautiful than Simon had been, and Andie was now a woman. A woman with the same hunger inside her that her sister had had. But, unlike Chrissy, Andie knew what happened when you indulged that hunger. She knew where following men like Poseidon led, and she wasn't going down that path. No matter how beautiful and rich he was.

He was in a dark charcoal suit today, with a white shirt and a tie of emerald silk that caught the green glints in his sea-blue eyes, and it was galling to realise how much she'd been playing down his attractiveness over the past couple of days. Telling herself that surely he hadn't been as beautiful as she'd thought, that it had been merely her fevered imagination.

But, no, he really was as handsome, and his presence made the waiting room seem even more dingy and depressing than it had been a few moments ago.

It was infuriating. She'd tried very hard, and with very limited resources, to get Chrissy's Hope up and running, and naturally all he had to do was step through the doors and it was as if a spell had been broken, revealing the truth that her efforts had been in vain. Nothing she could do with the funds she had was ever going to make this place a success.

She glared at him with open dislike. 'Thank you, but your appreciation isn't necessary. So please take your... token and leave.'

He made no move to do so, leaning against the reception desk instead, as if he was going to stand there all day. 'I allowed my PR department to let slip to the media that I was making a little trip, and I couldn't help but notice that several paparazzi followed me.' He glanced casually towards the front doors. 'I'm sure they'll be curious about why I'm here. I'm sure they'll want to investigate thoroughly and report.' He turned his gaze to the rest of the waiting room. 'They'll also note that I'm carrying a bunch of roses and will assume certain things based on that, since I'm not often seen carrying flowers. There'll be lots of speculation about who they're for and why.' Finally his blue gaze came back to hers. 'All of which adds up to the kind of publicity that thousands of companies pay millions for, wouldn't you say?'

Andie wanted desperately to refute every single one of his points. But she knew how the media worked as well as he did—she wasn't exactly a novice when it came to getting attention for a cause, after all—and he was right. He was infamous. The press loved him and followed him wherever he went. His presence here would cause a small sensation. The kind of sensation that could be very good for Chrissy's Hope indeed.

'Aren't you afraid they'll think you're an addict?' she asked, since it was all she could think of to say.

'No,' he said dismissively. 'And speculation is part of the point.' He glanced around the room once again and frowned. Then, before she could say anything, he crossed to the rickety table by the plastic chairs, still carrying the roses. 'Look,' he murmured. 'Your poor freesias are a bit the worse for wear.' He took the drooping freesias out of the vase and replaced them with the roses, arranging them in a few quick, deft motions. 'There,' he said. 'Much better.'

Gathering the freesias, he paused a minute, staring critically at the vase, then he plucked out a single rose stem. He glanced at one of his security guards, who was still standing at attention by the door, and the man instantly came over to him.

Poseidon handed him the freesias. 'Dispose of these, please,' he instructed, before strolling leisurely back to the reception desk, holding out the single rose to Andie.

There was a slightly wicked glint in his eyes…the same glint that she'd seen back in his office when they'd first met. It made her heart beat suddenly fast.

'You can surely allow yourself one,' he murmured.

That voice of his…so seductive. The devil himself surely had a voice like that, tempting mortals into sin.

The way Chrissy was tempted. And she gave in.

Her poor sister. But Andie wouldn't make that same mistake. She would resist.

Ignoring the rose, she stared at him. 'What is the point of this? Is it to manipulate me into agreeing to your stupid marriage idea?'

'If by "this" you mean the roses and my visit, then yes,' he agreed calmly, which took the wind out of her sails. 'But, as I said, it's also to generate some media interest in your service. A demonstration, if you will, of what I can do for you. After all, I merely need your presence at the altar and a bit of pretence. While you get...' He paused, looked around the sad waiting room once again, then back at her. 'You get the money and exposure that your very worthy service could use.'

He was correct and she didn't like it that he was. But her not liking it didn't make him any less right. She *could* use the money, and needed it badly. And if it was true, what he said about the publicity his visit here today would bring, then...well. She needed that too.

This is an opportunity. Don't waste it.

It *was* an opportunity—and one she couldn't allow to slip through her fingers. Yes, he was far too attractive for his own good, but that shouldn't get in the way of doing what was right for Chrissy's Hope. Also, he wasn't Simon and she wasn't Chrissy. She wouldn't make the same mistakes.

She would accept his proposal, get the sponsorship deal he'd promised and, with the money, turn Chrissy's Hope into a service that would save lives.

Decision made, Andie took a breath and then reached

for the rose Poseidon held out. And once again, even though she hadn't meant them to, her fingers brushed his, a surge of electricity arrowing down her spine, making her breath catch. Sparks of an answering heat glowed suddenly brilliant in his eyes, and for a second every thought in her head vanished.

He wants you, too.

'No,' he murmured, seemingly to himself, so low and quiet she barely heard.

'What did you say?' she asked, her own voice oddly husky.

'I said, are you going to agree, little siren?'

That wasn't at all what he'd said, but she suspected she knew why he'd said 'no' so emphatically. Since it wasn't a subject she wanted to talk about, or even think about, she let it go.

Instead, she put the rose carefully down on the reception desk and met his gaze. 'I'll need what you promised for Chrissy's Hope put into a contract and signed.'

Poseidon smiled, and instantly all her threat senses sprang into high alert. He reached inside his jacket, brought out an envelope, and handed it to her.

'Already done,' he said with some satisfaction. 'I had your lawyers okay it this morning.'

Of course he had. The man was arrogance personified, and then some.

Furious, she snatched the envelope from him—making very sure that this time their fingers didn't touch—and ripped it open. Sure enough, it was a full legal contract detailing her terms, and it had been signed by him.

'Check your email,' he added. 'Your lawyers have sent you their advice.'

'How did you even know who my lawyers were?' Andie demanded.

He lifted one powerful shoulder. 'I have excellent staff who easily found out which firm Chrissy's Hope uses. You can call them if you like, just to be certain.'

She wanted to change her mind, to refuse. She wanted to tell him to take his contract and leave and never come back, because this felt as if he'd somehow outmanoeuvred her and she hated that.

But she couldn't. She'd decided she was going to accept his marriage proposal and she couldn't keep letting her feelings get in the way.

'You're the most arrogant bastard I've ever had the misfortune to meet,' she said at last, because she had to vent those feelings somehow.

He kept right on smiling that devastating smile of his. 'What can I say? It's a gift.' He turned to the door. 'Call me when you've made your decision.'

She wanted to let him walk—she very much did. Because if what he'd said about his grandmother was correct, that he had to marry a woman of her choosing, then she was the woman who'd been chosen. He couldn't just find someone else if she refused. She had the power here, not him.

But it was pointless to wait when she already knew what she was going to do. What she'd been going to do the moment he'd suggested sponsoring Chrissy's Hope back in his office.

'Wait,' Andie said.

He stopped, his back to her, a tall, powerful figure in the shabby waiting room. His head turned slightly. 'Yes?'

'Okay,' she said. 'Yes. I'll marry you.'

He nodded, with his head half turned away. She couldn't see his face. 'I'll send a car for you tomorrow,' he said. 'We can go over the details then.'

Then, before she could make any further comment, he walked out.

CHAPTER FOUR

POSEIDON SAT AT the table on the terrace of his penthouse apartment in the warm summer sun, studying the media reports his PR department had forwarded to him of yesterday's little visit to Andromeda.

There were pictures of him exiting his limo and going into the shabby offices of her addiction service, carrying the big bunch of roses, along with gossipy articles about what the roses meant and who they were for, and what Chrissy's Hope was, and why he was there.

It had been a relatively small performance in the greater scheme of things—a demonstration, as he'd told her, of the kind of attention he could command and what that could potentially mean for her service. Yet it seemed to have had the desired effect, both with the media and with Andromeda.

She'd been hostile initially, as he'd known she would be, standing behind her clearly second-hand reception desk, back straight, chin lifted, as if she was the empress of all she surveyed.

It had been sexy, he had to admit, even though she was fully clothed this time. A pity. Then again, the jeans and T-shirt she'd worn had outlined her curves just as effectively as the body paint, and those curves had been just as delicious as he'd remembered. Her riot of red-gold curls had been gathered in a loose ponytail at her nape, and there'd been the sweetest little scattering of freckles across her nose.

But her eyes had been as sharp as green glass, and just as full of dislike as they had been a few days earlier, and he'd known a second's doubt as he'd handed her the roses. Which was strange. He'd never doubted himself before with a woman—never.

The doubt had only deepened when she'd taken the rose from him and her fingers had once again brushed his. And he'd felt heat surge between them—the same heat that had seared him in that moment in his office a few days earlier. A gut-punch of attraction that he'd found impossible to ignore.

The 'no' had escaped him before he'd been able to think better of it, a reminder to himself that he'd made the decision not to touch her. But she'd heard him. Had she known what he'd meant? He hadn't been sure, but he hadn't bothered to explain. People could use desire to get anything they wanted out of you if you weren't careful, so she didn't need to know he found her beautiful or in any way desirable. That was a power he didn't want to give her. Especially a woman like her, a woman who cared deeply and passionately for her cause, and who would no doubt be willing to do anything for its benefit.

You're manipulating her the way Michel manipulated you. You do realise that, don't you?

No, he'd already told himself that wasn't what he was doing. He'd merely put together a proposal for their mutual benefit, that was all. He wasn't forcing her to sign anything if she didn't want to.

The memory of that dingy, shabby waiting room drifted through his consciousness, with its plastic chairs and the drooping flowers, and the pathetic pictures on the walls, obviously torn from a magazine. She'd clearly tried to make it welcoming, but had only succeeded in making it depressing—and, honestly, the real question was why it had taken her so long to agree to his marriage proposal, given how desperately she needed the money.

Yet she had agreed, finally, and he could still feel the thrill of satisfaction that had gone through him in that moment. A hungry kind of satisfaction, which had disturbed him so much he'd thought it better to leave rather than hash out the details there and then. Satisfaction was allowable, but he had not liked that hunger. It spoke of need, of that void inside him that his father's death had left and that Michel had stepped into.

He wouldn't ever let himself feel that again.

'Mr Teras?'

He looked up from his laptop to see his housekeeper standing in the doorway to the terrace. 'Has Miss Lane arrived, Molly?'

'Yes.'

'Good. Show her out here, if you would.'

Molly nodded, then disappeared back into the penthouse interior.

Andromeda had arrived, as he'd instructed.

He felt an odd leap of something that couldn't possibly be anticipation—because why? He should feel satisfied, yes, as once this marriage issue was over and done with, and the issue of Dimitra's shares settled, he could return to what really mattered, which was his shipping empire. Yet he couldn't deny he was looking forward to seeing Andromeda again.

He wasn't sure why, since she was nothing but sharp edges, and too much dislike could get tiresome, yet there was something about her that fascinated him. Sexual attraction, of course, but also the fire in her that seemed to burn so hotly and so bright. She didn't strike him as being a woman who was afraid of anything. She certainly wasn't afraid of him, and why that was so damn attractive he couldn't say.

He glanced around the terrace to make sure all was in order. Molly had prepared a wonderful morning tea with scones and jam and some clotted cream. The day was warm, too. The scent of lavender from the large pots lining the terrace reminded him of the Teras estate on the island kingdom where he'd grown up.

After Michel he'd left the island, and had avoided it like the plague ever since, only returning once when Dimitra had demanded his presence to lay down her marriage challenge. It wasn't the memories that bothered him—not at all. He never thought of that time. It was only that he'd outgrown the place, that was all. Michel had died a decade ago, and he had no hold on Poseidon—not any more.

'Mr Teras,' Molly said from the doorway. 'Miss Lane is here.'

Poseidon dragged his thoughts away from the past and looked up. Andromeda stood beside his housekeeper wearing a light, airy, flowing dress the colour of spring leaves. Her hair was loose, her red-gold curls a riot down her back, and she wore a quantity of thin silver bracelets around one wrist. Her green eyes, echoing the colour of her dress, met his, and he felt it yet again, that punch of desire, so strong it stole his breath.

She was so beautiful. Had she worn that dress for his benefit? Surely she had. The colour made her skin look pearlescent and her eyes glow. While the loose fit hid her curves, the fabric was so filmy he could see the delicate lines of the pretty lace bra and knickers she wore underneath it.

'Thank you, Molly,' he said, struggling to keep his voice even as he rose from his seat. 'Welcome, Andromeda.' He moved around the table and pulled out the chair opposite his, gesturing to it. 'Please, join me for some tea.'

Molly withdrew, while Andromeda eyed him with her usual suspicion.

He was going to need to do something about that suspicion, because Dimitra would certainly pick up on it—she was sharp like that—and that would expose his little charade.

He smiled. 'There's no need to look at me with such distrust, little siren. I'm only offering tea and scones, not heroin.'

'Don't call me that. I gave you my name.'

He lifted a brow. 'You'd rather not be called after a beautiful woman with a seductive voice?'

Andromeda's gaze narrowed even further. 'I suppose it's better than being called Poseidon.'

He laughed—because, really, no one had made fun of his name since he was a child. No one would dare. Yet of course *she* would.

'There's nothing wrong with being named after the god of the sea,' he said. 'Especially when one owns a highly successful shipping company. A bit disconcerting, I suppose, given your name is Androm—'

'Yes, yes, I know,' she snapped.

Her cheeks had gone pink, which intrigued him. What was she embarrassed about? Or was she angry? Perhaps both?

'But I'm not a helpless princess. And you're not a god.'

'Am I not? The women who scream my name in bed might disagree with you.'

Her flush deepened even more. 'You're the most arrogant—'

'Bastard you've ever met,' he interrupted. 'Yes, so you've said.' He gestured to the chair again. 'Come and sit down. It's perfectly safe to step onto the terrace. Both the floor and this chair are very sturdy.'

She rolled her eyes, but stepped onto the terrace and came over to where he stood behind the chair, stopping next to it. 'You don't have to stand there,' she said. 'I can push my own chair in.'

He looked down at her, since she was shorter than he was by nearly a head, very conscious of how close she was and of her delicate scent…unexpectedly sweet, like vanilla.

You should not let her get this near to you.

No, he should not. Especially when he could now see her bra and knickers even more clearly through the fabric of her dress. He'd thought that perhaps it had been deliberate, but now he'd changed his mind. She'd flushed so deeply when he'd mentioned women screaming his name, maybe she wasn't aware.

'And you can stop looking at my underwear too,' she said, plucking the thought right out of his head.

It took him off-guard so completely that he actually found himself protesting. 'I wasn't looking at your underwear.'

'Of course you were. This dress is a bit see-through, but I had to wear it because all my other clothes were in the wash.' She gave him a very penetrating look. 'And you're a man. You can't help yourself.'

For a long moment Poseidon was so confounded by this bit of truth that he couldn't think of a word to say. Her green gaze was steady, disapproving, as if she didn't care about the fact that her dress was see-through. As if it didn't bother her at all. As if *he* didn't bother her, despite the way she was blushing like a sunset. And suddenly he was seized with an urge to make her bothered, to shake her the way she'd shaken him.

'Were your other clothes really in the wash?' he

drawled. 'Or is that dress and the pretty little bra and knicker set for my benefit?'

Instantly emerald sparks glittered in her eyes and her chin lifted. 'Hardly. Why would they be?'

He found he'd taken a step towards her, closing what little distance there was between them, even though he knew it was a stupid idea.

'Because you want my attention, little siren,' he said. 'Why else?'

'I do not.' The pink in her cheeks had deepened still further, bringing out the brilliant clear green of her eyes. She didn't step back, didn't give an inch of ground. 'I can't think of anything worse.'

'Really?' He lifted his hand and cupped her cheek, her skin soft beneath his fingers. 'My attention is the worst thing you can think of?'

She went very still as he touched her, and he heard her breath catch. Her eyes had gone wide, staring up into his, and he thought she'd pull away, but she didn't. She only stood there, looking up at him as her leaf-green eyes slowly darkened into deep emerald. Time seemed to slow, the air around them becoming thick and crackling with static. Her skin was warm and smooth, like satin pressing against his palm, and he couldn't help sliding his hand along her jaw, into the silky softness of her glorious hair, tilting her head back slightly.

Again, she made no move to pull away, only staring up at him as if mesmerised. Then, suddenly, she rose up on her toes and pressed her mouth to his.

* * *

Andie didn't know what had come over her. She'd ar-rived at his ludicrously expensive city penthouse, her loins girded for battle over this marriage deal, only to find him lounging at a table on the terrace, looking so ridiculously sexy she almost couldn't tear her gaze away.

He looked more casual today, in a plain black busi-ness shirt and grey suit trousers, no tie. His shirt was open at the neck and she'd immediately fixated on the smooth, olive skin of his throat and the pulse that beat there, strong and regular. His hypnotic gaze had met hers, and the same heat that had gripped her the day before, when he'd handed her the contract and their fin-gers had brushed, had gripped her again.

It wasn't fair that he should be so fiercely attractive and it wasn't fair that she should notice. It wasn't fair that she'd found it so hard to resist the draw of him and she had to. She was furious with herself and her physical reaction to him. Furious with him, too, for calling her 'little siren' and looking at her with that knowing blue gaze. Her dress was slightly see-through—yes, she knew that—but it was hot, and she'd wanted to wear some-thing light, and her only clean underwear had been dark.

He shouldn't have been looking at her that way and she shouldn't have liked it. She shouldn't have let slip that she knew he'd been looking. She shouldn't have snapped at him…shouldn't have reacted when he'd taunted her about his attention being the worst thing that she could think of.

She shouldn't have allowed her anger to get the better of her.

Because if she'd controlled it...if she hadn't risen to his bait...he wouldn't have laid his large, warm palm against her cheek, and all the breath wouldn't have left her body. She wouldn't have felt his touch like a lightning bolt, igniting something inside her and making it roar into life, like dry grass to a lit match.

She wouldn't have completely lost her head, wanting to shock him the way he'd shocked her, and risen up on her toes to kiss his beautiful mouth.

But she'd done all of those things. And now it was too late.

Because after a moment of stillness, when she could sense that she'd surprised him, that mouth of his opened, and his fingers tightened in her hair, and he was kissing her, and she was lost.

He tasted of everything dark and sinful and delicious...everything that she knew was bad for her...everything she'd been running from since Chrissy had died. The hunger that she'd always known was inside her, that somehow he'd brought into full, aching life, had her in its grip, and she had her hands on his chest, her palms pressed to his shirt, feeling the hard muscle and heat beneath it before she could think straight.

He made a rough sound and his fingers tightened in her hair, his mouth opening, his tongue exploring her, hot and demanding. She hadn't kissed anyone before, had no idea what she was doing, but she followed his lead, kissing him back as hungrily as he was kissing her.

She felt desperate, taken out of herself, and the only things that mattered were the pulsing ache that had started up between her thighs and the frantic need to touch his bare skin, feel his warmth.

Her fingers curled into his shirt as she pressed herself against him. The heat of his rock-hard body was like a furnace. Some part of her was screaming that this was a terrible idea, that this was the same trap Chrissy had fallen into, but she ignored it. It felt as if her every thought was fracturing under the pressure of her hunger, and she wouldn't be able to think clearly until she'd sated it.

He slid one arm around her waist, holding her to him, and the fingers in her hair opened, so he was cradling the back of her head. He'd gentled the kiss, which was not what she wanted, and she clutched at him, trying to follow his mouth as he lifted it from hers.

'Little siren,' he murmured against her lips. His deep voice had gone rough, as if he too felt the same hunger she did. 'Keep kissing me like that and we're going to end up in my bed, and I need you to be very sure that's where you want to be before that happens.'

Someone was breathing fast and hard and Andie was suddenly aware that it was her, and also that she was shaking. Her mouth felt hot and sensitive, and the rich, woody, spicy scent of him had lodged somewhere deep inside her.

In his bed. Did she want that?

Of course you do. You're just like Chrissy...too hun-

gry...and if you're not careful you'll get into the same spiral she did.

Poseidon Teras was everything she was supposed to avoid, not throw herself at. How could she have forgotten that so completely?

Andie pushed herself away from him, turning so he wouldn't see how hard it was to pull herself together. He was silent, making no move to touch her as she took a couple of deep breaths, struggling for control.

'I'm sorry,' she said. 'That was my fault. I shouldn't have kissed you.'

Because it *was* her fault. She'd let herself get too angry and it had backfired spectacularly.

Bracing herself for him to say something insufferably smug and arrogant, she was surprised when he said, 'No, you shouldn't have.'

She glanced at him, because she'd clearly offended him—which was strange, because surely women throwing themselves at him wasn't anything new.

Yet it wasn't offence burning in his eyes, but fire. An intense blue flame that made the hunger inside her pull on its leash.

'We have chemistry, Andromeda.' His voice was flat, with no humour in it, no trace of his usual charming smile or dry tone. 'And it's volatile. So if you don't want to end up flat on your back with me inside you, perhaps it would be best if you kept your distance.'

She shivered, the image his blunt words had conjured up making her dry-mouthed with want, but she forced the feeling aside and nodded. He didn't say anything else, moving past her to sit down at the other end of the table as if nothing untoward had happened.

Yet she felt as if the world had shifted on its axis… as if the ground under her feet wasn't as steady as she'd thought and now every step was suspect.

What had she done? Why? What was so special about him that made her forget every rule she'd given herself since Chrissy had died?

That kiss… She'd tasted something in him, something passionate and raw that had been the same hunger she'd felt herself. It was as if some part of her had recognised a part of him and seen a kindred spirit. Except that made no sense. He was nothing like her—nothing at all. He cared about nothing and no one, and the kiss had probably been a cynical way to—

You *kissed him. And he was the one who stopped it.*

He hadn't taken advantage of the moment by using her hunger against her in some way. Unlike Simon, who'd used Chrissy's infatuation with him to draw her deeper and deeper into his world.

Still, that didn't make Poseidon a good man—though he was right about one thing. They did have chemistry, and she really did need to keep her distance from him.

Unless you want to end up in his bed?

No, she *didn't* want that. Not at all.

Slowly, she moved over to the chair he'd been standing behind and sat down.

His beautiful face was drawn in hard lines, his finely carved mouth—that beautiful mouth she'd just kissed— was unsmiling. He looked stern. And there was a definite chill in his blue eyes…a stormy blue with no green at all.

That kiss had been a mistake and they both knew it.

'Tea?' he asked, his voice very neutral. 'A scone, perhaps?'

'No, thank you.' She wished her own voice didn't sound quite so husky, but there was nothing she could do about it.

He didn't insist, pouring himself tea and adding a touch of milk. Then he picked up one of the fluffy-looking scones in a long-fingered hand and put it on a plate, deftly cutting it in half.

'So,' he said, as he began to butter it in a leisurely fashion. 'You understand that before our marriage a period of courtship will need to take place? In order to convince my darling grandmother that this is a real marriage.'

It was clear they weren't going to talk about that kiss again, which was good, since she definitely didn't want to talk about it. But, still, it was difficult to get her mind back on track when her mouth still felt sensitised, and her heartbeat was going like a drum, and the ache between her thighs was insistent.

She wanted to get angry, because anger was familiar, but she couldn't seem to grab hold of it.

A good thing. That's not useful to you now.

It was true. Letting it control her around him was not a good idea, and, besides, they needed to talk about this whole marriage deal. No point starting off negotiations with fury.

'Yes,' she said. 'I understand.'

'Good.' He picked up a silver bowl and proceeded to spread jam on the scone. 'So, I propose a few public appearances, so the media are clear we are an item. Two should do it, I would think. Then I'll have my PR people issue a press release about our upcoming wedding.'

Andromeda felt something inside her tense. *Public appearances.* She supposed it made sense, since they were supposed to be actually in love, but she didn't like it. What would it mean for Chrissy's Hope if she was seen with him? Exposure, yes, but for an addiction service, and he was a notorious playboy. How would that look?

'Can we not just get married?' she asked, trying not to sound reluctant. 'Do we need to have any public appearances?'

'Dimitra is by nature suspicious,' he said. 'And I fear that me marrying you a week after she chose you for me won't be a convincing enough love story for her.'

He'd finished with the jam and now picked up another bowl full of delicious-looking clotted cream.

'She will also insist on us marrying in the church on the island kingdom where I grew up, by the way. It's in the Mediterranean…not too far by plane.'

Andromeda's vision of a quickie wedding at a register office quickly vanished. 'So, you're talking about…?'

'A white gown, walking down the aisle, vicars, heavenly choirs—yes, the whole nine yards.' He gently laid a scoop of cream on his scone. 'Necessary theatre in this instance.'

Andie had never envisaged herself as a bride, never had dreams of a white wedding, never thought she'd walk down the aisle. Not after her sister had died. Simon had given Chrissy vague hints about taking their relationship to 'the next level', or so she'd told Andie, and Chrissy had been starry-eyed about it. She'd been the one with the white wedding dreams, thinking Simon was the love of her life.

Except he hadn't been. He'd taken her to parties, given her drugs, and then suggested that sleeping with his friends would be an easy and quick way for her to earn money. And that had been the end of Chrissy's dreams.

The fury inside Andie at the injustice of it all, which had been burning sullenly for years, flickered back into life again. But this time, instead of reaching for it, she tried to ignore it.

Chrissy wouldn't get a white wedding, but if Andie did what Poseidon wanted, and participated in his 'necessary theatre', then she could help other women like Chrissy—women in desperate situations. That was more important than her rage.

So all she said was, 'Okay. I can do that. So what kind of appearances are we talking about here?'

'Probably a couple of events. Hopefully the exposure will have some positive implications for your service.'

'Yes, I'm sure being seen with a notorious playboy billionaire will help my service,' she couldn't help saying tartly.

He gave her a cool look. 'I'm not an addict.'

'But you're also not known for your abstemious lifestyle.'

'Does it matter? There's no such thing as bad publicity, Andromeda, or haven't you heard?'

He was right. Chrissy's Hope needed the exposure, regardless of who he was, and without him being who he was she'd be back at square one.

She let out a breath. 'I don't want it to look like I'm selling out.'

He'd gone back to his scone, but now he looked up from it, and for a second amusement lit his blue eyes. 'Oh, dear. Have I become "the man"?'

He'd been so serious just before that his sudden amusement now caught her off-guard, almost coaxing a brief smile of her own out of her. It felt unfamiliar to smile. To find something even mildly funny. In fact, she couldn't remember the last time she had. Everything had been so very serious since Chrissy had died, and so desperate. It still felt that way—mainly because it *was* desperate. Other lives were at stake here and she couldn't joke about it.

Except she couldn't resist saying, 'If I was working for you, then you would indeed be "the man". But since I'm not, you're just "a" man.'

His expression relaxed, his mouth curving into a suggestion of that devastating smile, hints of fascinating green glinting in his eyes, and she felt something shift inside her. Because it was a natural smile, as if she'd surprised it out of him, and for some reason that made her feel a little less desperate and a little less angry.

'I'm not just *a* man, little siren,' he said. 'I'm the god

of the sea.' He pushed the plate with the scone on it in her direction. 'Here, have a scone.'

The god of the sea indeed. She wanted to tell him he was being ridiculous, and that she didn't want a scone, but for some reason she reached out and pulled the plate closer. She hadn't had any lunch and the scone did look delicious.

'So how will you be at acting as if you're madly in love with me?' he asked, leaning back in his chair and watching her. 'As opposed to, say, acting as if you want to bury my body where no one will ever find it.'

She eyed him. 'I don't look at you like that.'

'Perhaps not,' he murmured. 'At least not all the time.'

Just for a moment the reminder of that kiss burned between them, hot and hungry and desperate. And, no, she hadn't looked at him as if she wanted to kill him then. She'd looked at him as if she wanted to eat him alive.

Her cheeks felt hot, but she wasn't going to look away or act as if it hadn't happened. 'If you're referring to the kiss, that was a one-off thing.'

He shrugged. 'Then you'll have to pretend.'

Andie let out an irritated breath. This was going to be even more annoying than she'd thought. She wasn't good at pretending, because it felt dishonest, and she hated dishonesty.

Is it pretending, though? You do want him.

She wished she could deny it, but that would be lying to herself, and that was dishonest too. So, yes, she did want him. But that wasn't love, and pretending to be in love with Poseidon felt wrong. It was a deception, and it wasn't just the media they were deceiving, but also his grandmother.

'I don't like lying to people,' she said, just so he was clear. 'And this is one big lie.'

'Yes,' he agreed. 'It is. But in this instance it's a small lie for the greater good. No one will be hurt by it, for example, and certainly for you lives could be saved.'

This was all very true and, loath as she was to admit it, he did have a point. 'Your grandmother will be hurt if she finds out,' she said.

'But she won't find out if we're careful.' He nodded to the scone. 'You're hungry. I can tell. And that scone is looking very good to you right now, isn't it?'

'Yes, I suppose so.'

'So…' He smiled 'Look at me as if I'm that scone.'

Andie blinked. 'What?'

'You're eyeing that scone as if you can't wait to eat it. That's the way a woman should look at the man she loves, hmm?' He tilted his head, and the blue of his eyes intensified. 'Alternatively, you could look at me the way you did just before you kissed me.'

And it was back—the hot, bright crackling energy that arced between them, making her breath catch, her heart beat far too fast, and the pressure between her thighs ache.

'Yes,' he breathed, his gaze holding her captive. 'Just like that.'

She should look away, and yet she couldn't bring herself to. It felt like a concession, and she wasn't prepared to give him one, not when he was so powerful already.

So she held his gaze and kept on holding it, daring him to look away first.

'Andromeda,' he murmured, her name sounding deep and rough. 'You are playing with fire.'

'Why? Is it yourself you don't trust or me?'

'Do you want to be in my bed?'

His voice wound around her, the rough heat in it making her shiver.

'I warn you that's where you're going to end up if you keep looking at me like that.'

A dark shiver went through her, and a kind of recklessness followed on behind it. He was so sure of himself, and so certain about what she wanted and what she didn't. But what did he know? He knew nothing about her.

'Is that a promise or a threat?' she asked.

The look in his eyes became focused, intent. 'What do you want it to be?'

You are *playing with fire.*

Maybe she was, but that wild recklessness was deepening its claws in her, making her want to push and keep pushing, prove her power over him. And she did have power over him—she could see that. His knuckles were white where he gripped the arms of his chair, and a muscle jumped in the side of his strong jaw. He looked as if he was struggling to hold himself back, and he was so unbearably sexy like this she could hardly stand it.

His intensity drew her like a moth to a flame.

The same way Simon drew you. The same way he drew Chrissy.

She tore her gaze from his as the thought hit her, her heart thumping uncomfortably loud in her ears. By looking away she'd conceded ground, she knew. She'd given up a piece of her power. But continuing to stare at him was madness.

She needed to get out—leave. Get some space. Figure out how to deal with him. Because getting angry wasn't it. It only led her further into the trap.

She risked a brief glance across the table at him, and once again she found him looking back. Their gazes clashed, held.

'I think you should probably leave,' Poseidon said, in a voice that was deeper and rougher than she remembered.

'Yes,' she said hoarsely. 'I think you're probably right.'

So she thrust her chair back, got to her feet, turned around and left.

Before she did something stupid.

CHAPTER FIVE

POSEIDON STOOD OUTSIDE the front door of the rundown flat where Andromeda lived, his limo waiting at the kerb. Normally he'd have sent his driver to announce his arrival, but tonight he wanted to meet Andromeda at the door himself.

He was here to collect her for their first appearance together—a child poverty fundraiser at the Natural History Museum—and they'd already had a fraught phone call a couple of days earlier, when he'd given her the details of the event, and she'd argued with him about the outfit he'd sent her, since he was sure she didn't have a wardrobe full of event wear at the ready.

He'd known she'd argue with him and he'd relished it, even though he knew he shouldn't. Even though he knew encouraging the sparks they drew from each other was a mistake. She'd agreed at last that a dress from a high street chain store wasn't going to cut it at a glittering, star-studded event, but then tried to insist on choosing her own dress. He'd offered her an alternative, her modelling a selection for him, which she'd declined. It had only been after a good fifteen minutes of back and forth that she'd accepted that, since he attended these events all the time, he had a better idea of what kind of dress was appropriate than she did.

He'd taken his time choosing the perfect gown. Green, naturally, for her eyes, and simple—nothing that would detract from her glorious figure or her hair. Silk, of course, with a drape, and a sheen that would complement her skin and feel nice to wear.

Eventually he'd settled on something beautiful and had it sent to her, and had braced himself for yet more argument. But the only reply he'd received was that it had arrived and it fitted. That was all.

Now, he stood on the doorstep, every muscle in his body drawn so tight with anticipation it was almost painful. Though, to be fair, he'd felt that way ever since the glory that had been her kiss a week earlier. He'd never had a woman tie him up in such knots before, and with only a kiss. Quite honestly, he couldn't understand it. Her kiss had been unpractised and uncertain, a little hesitant. Yet after that first moment it had blossomed into something so hot and sweet he hadn't been able to resist her. She hadn't tasted like citrus, but strawberries, and then she'd pressed all those delectable curves against him, and he'd felt the flame of her burn bright between his hands—

No. He had to stop going over it. He'd been doing so for days, the memory catching him at the most inappropriate times, in meetings with shareholders, while he was trying to concentrate on reports, or troubleshooting staffing issues. It was getting tiresome, especially when he knew he had only himself to blame. He hadn't been going to touch her, yet he'd cupped her cheek in his hand, unable to resist the temptation, and her skin had been so warm. Then her eyes had darkened. He'd been going to pull away, put some distance between them, but then she'd risen on her toes and pressed her mouth to his before he'd even known what she was doing.

It had shocked him. Then he'd been shocked again as the most intense heat had risen inside him, a hunger he'd had no name for, which had reminded him of long ago. It should have been enough for him to step away, but he hadn't. There had been something between them more than physical attraction, something deeper, and he hadn't be able to resist.

A mistake.

And a hell of a mistake. Because now he couldn't stop thinking about it, about her, and about that kiss and how he wanted more.

You weren't going to sleep with her, remember?

Poseidon bit off a curse and pressed her doorbell again, impatient. He definitely *wasn't* going to sleep with her, and that was all there was to it. Her kiss might have set him on fire, and he might still be burning even a week later, but those flames weren't going anywhere. He'd bank the embers until he could let them burn at a later date, with someone more appropriate. Someone who wasn't her.

Finally, the door was pulled open and Andromeda stood in the doorway. All the breath left his body.

He'd known she'd look beautiful in the gown he'd picked, but he hadn't known she'd look *quite* so beautiful.

The gown was simple, cut on the bias so it hugged

her figure, curving around her breasts, hips, and thighs before swirling out into full skirts just above her knee. Tiny straps over her pale shoulders held it up, and the neckline draped beautifully over her breasts. The rich silk was the same clear leaf-green as her eyes and, as he'd thought, she looked like a wood nymph or the goddess of spring personified. Her hair was loose in artfully styled curls down her back, framing her angular face in the most flattering way.

Poseidon couldn't think of a woman he'd escorted anywhere who was lovelier.

She gave him a challenging stare, as if daring him to make some comment, her sharp chin lifted, but even the expression on her face couldn't detract from the overall effect of the gown.

'You're beautiful,' he said simply. 'You take my breath away.'

Her lush mouth parted and her eyes widened, a blush rising to her cheeks.

He was a practised flirt, and yet he was aware that there had been nothing practised about what he'd just said. And he meant it. She *had* taken his breath away. And that was a dangerous thing to admit. It was honest. Perhaps it was too honest.

'Thank you,' she said, and glanced down at the clutch in her hand, fussing with it a moment, before looking up at him again. 'Well? Shall we go?'

He'd flustered her, he could see. Good. If he'd slipped up with an honesty he hadn't meant to reveal, she could be bothered by it in a way she hadn't expected.

Wordlessly, he held out an arm and, to his surprise, she laid one small hand on it without protest, letting him escort her to the limo. He opened the door and she got in, then he followed, shutting it behind him and enclosing them both in the warm interior.

He was almost unbearably conscious of her sitting next to him, not touching, but close, one silk-covered thigh next to his. He could feel her warmth, the light vanilla scent of her perfume wrapping sweetly around him.

He forced himself to ignore it. Bringing her to the gala was for show and for show only. Nothing would be happening between them.

And when she looks at you the way she looked at you on the terrace last week? Just before she kissed you? How are you going to resist then?

He just would. He wasn't a teenage boy at the mercy of his hormones. He was a grown man who'd been controlling himself easily for years, and one pretty activist wasn't going to change that.

'I meant what I said,' he murmured into the heavy silence. 'You *do* look beautiful in the gown.'

She pulled a face. 'It's too tight, and the fabric pulls weirdly, and it's also far too expensive. You could have let me choose the dress myself.'

'It's true, I could,' he agreed. 'But in the end I decided on the more irritating path and chose it for you. You're welcome.'

She snorted and looked away out of the window. 'I'm not keeping it. I'm going to donate it.'

Poseidon stared at her, thinking about the shabby

waiting room of Chrissy's Hope and the rundown exterior of her flat. The dress she'd worn the last time he'd seen her because all her other clothes were in the wash.

She didn't have much, he suspected, and yet instead of being concerned about herself, she expended all her energy crusading on behalf of others. He wondered why. He wondered why she was so angry, so full of fury and sharp edges and ferocity. It was for her sister, he was sure.

Don't get interested. You're not supposed to care.

He didn't. He was just…curious, and their time together would go easier if they weren't at each other's throats all the time.

'You're allowed to have nice things, you know,' he murmured.

She turned her head. 'What do you mean? What nice things?'

'The dress. It's yours. If you like it, keep it.'

'Why would I want to?' There was a belligerent look on her face. 'It's completely inappropriate. Also, I have nowhere to wear it, and I—'

'You like it, don't you?' Poseidon interrupted as the realisation caught him.

A wild rush of colour stained her cheeks. 'No, I don't. Why would you say that?'

'Because you're expending so much effort denying it.' He was conscious of a certain satisfaction rolling through him, that she liked what he'd chosen for her after all. 'It does make me want to know why, though. After all, the entire world won't collapse if you like wearing a pretty silk gown. Is it because it's expensive or because I bought it for you?'

A shadow moved across her face, gone so fast he wasn't sure he'd seen it at all.

She looked down at the green silk clutch in her hands. 'You wouldn't understand.'

It wasn't a denial this time. Interesting...

'Try me,' he said.

She was silent a moment, still staring down at the clutch in her hands. Then she said, 'My sister and I came from nothing. Our mother was a single parent and we never had much money. Chrissy hated being poor. She wanted more—something better, something that wasn't a council flat and a life spent slaving away in a dead-end job. So when she met a man—Simon—who showered her with expensive presents, who partied with celebrities, who showed her a world she wanted to be part of... Well, she fell for him.' Slowly, Andromeda's lashes lifted and she looked at him. 'And in the end it killed her.'

The words were a shock, as she'd no doubt intended them to be. He also didn't miss the accusatory note in her voice.

'I had nothing to do with your sister's death,' he said. 'I told you that.'

'It was still your yacht. And how are you any different from Simon? He bought her pretty dresses, jewellery, holidays in Paris and Rome. Took her on private planes and to exclusive nightclubs where they only drank the best champagne. Then he introduced her to the best drugs and got her hooked, before pimping her out to all his friends.'

She threw the words like stones, as if he was a glass-house and she was trying to break each and every one of his windows. He could understand why. He'd some-how become emblematic of the man who'd hurt Chrissy, who'd led her to her death, hadn't he? And now Androm-eda was taking her anger out on him.

'You think I'm the same kind of man?' he asked, just to be clear. 'Because I'm rich and I bought you a gown?'

She was sitting rigid in the seat, green eyes sharp, and she didn't flinch. 'They were all like that—all his rich, powerful friends. None of them helped her on that yacht when she took that overdose. And none of them cared.'

He shouldn't want to prove to her that he wasn't like them. What did her opinion matter? Yet somehow it was important to him that she understood that he *was* differ-ent. But also…was this really about the gown? Or did it have more to do with the fact that she liked it and didn't want to admit it? Was she afraid? Was that it? And, if so, what was she afraid of?

He studied her a moment. 'Liking the gown I bought you doesn't automatically lead directly to an overdose on my yacht—you know that, don't you?'

Her colour deepened and he knew that he'd got it right. She *was* afraid, and not of him.

'Firstly,' he went on, not waiting for her to waste time denying it, 'while it's true I am rich, and fairly power-ful, and I do like to buy women pretty dresses and jew-ellery, I don't do drugs. Nor have I ever bought drugs for anyone else. Secondly, I have never pimped anyone out to my friends, and if I knew of anyone who had I'd take him out into a dark alleyway and show him the error of his ways in painful detail.'

She took a little breath, her jaw tight. 'I've only got your word for that.'

He still couldn't understand why it was important that she believe him. Perhaps it was only that she had to stop thinking he was the devil incarnate every time he opened his mouth so that this little game they were playing for Dimitra's benefit would work.

'I know. Nevertheless, it's true. I'm not Simon, Andromeda. And you're not your sister either.'

She kept on staring at him. The atmosphere in the limo was taut and crackling with a familiar electricity. Then she tore her gaze away and looked down at her hands again.

'I'm still going to donate the dress.'

Did that mean she believed him? The fact that she'd changed the subject was proof enough, he supposed. She didn't like giving in, that was clear.

'You can send the dress on a rocket ship to the moon for all I care,' he said. 'But I suggest not biting my head off every time we meet. Why make this harder than it needs to be?'

She was silent for a long moment and then, slowly, the tension began to bleed out of her. 'You're right,' she said at last. 'I'll try.' She lifted her gaze to his again. 'So. What do I have to do at this event?'

He was tempted to ask her more about her sister,

though again he wasn't sure why, when getting to know her wasn't part of this deal. He only needed her presence, not her history, so he let it go.

'You don't have to do anything but stand next to me and look adoring.'

She rolled her eyes. 'Really?'

'We do have to look as if we're in love, little siren. And generally people who are in love look at each other with some degree of adoration…' He hesitated, and then added, 'They don't tend to stand apart from each other either.'

Another blush stole across her cheeks. 'What are you saying?'

The strange intensity that had been gripping him all week coiled through him once again at the thought of getting close to her. Of touching her. Because of course he'd have to touch her. They were supposed to look as if they were in love, after all.

'You'll probably have to stand close to me.' He tried to keep the intensity out of his voice. 'And I'll have to put my arm around you, hold your hand, et cetera.'

They were only stage directions, not promises. Because that's all it was, a performance for the media and Dimitra, nothing more. Yet…the anticipation that gripped him at the thought of her touch, and of him touching her, was making all the blood in his body rush below his belt.

Her eyes glittered like jewels in the dim interior of the limo. 'Will I have to kiss you?'

A shock went through him. He hadn't expected her

to bring up that subject, especially given how flustered she'd been by the kiss she'd given him on the terrace. And she *had* been flustered. After all, he'd been the one to stop it, not her.

You could have had her in your bed and you both know it.

She wouldn't have objected if he'd picked her up and carried her inside—not given how she'd followed his mouth as he'd tried to break it off, her fingers curling into his shirt. It had only been when he'd given her time to think that she'd pushed herself away from him.

He should do the same thing now. Look away, break the hold this chemistry had on them both. Yet he didn't.

'I should think so,' he murmured. 'The media will probably insist.' He lifted one brow. 'Is that going to be a problem for you?'

Of course it was going to be a problem for her, but Andie wasn't going to admit that to him. Not when he sat next to her with all the casual arrogance that was a part of him, looking particularly devastating in black evening clothes that suited his dark, fallen angel looks to perfection.

Her heart was beating so loudly she could hardly hear anything else, and the warmth of his body and the scent of his aftershave was making her dizzy and dry-mouthed with want.

She shouldn't have been so prickly with him. He was right about not biting his head off every time they met— not if they were supposed to look as if they were in love.

But she'd been on edge the whole week, and seeing him again hadn't done anything to make it easier.

She hadn't been able to stop thinking about the kiss, no matter what she'd been doing, and the calls she'd been getting from the media with questions about her 'relationship' with Poseidon Teras hadn't helped. She'd been issuing a steady stream of 'no comments' to each one, except when they asked about Chrissy's Hope, and she was tired of it. She was tired of thinking about how his mouth had tasted and how his body had felt when she'd pressed herself against him, and how much she'd wanted to bury her face in his neck and inhale him.

Their argument on the phone about the event, and his high-handedness in buying her a dress, had helped let off a bit of steam—until the dress had arrived, that was, and had been the most beautiful thing she'd ever seen in her entire life.

She remembered watching Chrissy dress in the pretty things that Simon had bought for her, secretly burning with envy, wishing she had someone who would buy her such lovely things too. She'd cut that envy out of her heart after Chrissy had died. She had told herself that she didn't need any expensive, pretty items, that she could get a perfectly lovely dress from the charity shop down the road. But as soon as the gown had been delivered all those firm instructions to herself had gone out of the window.

The silk had felt so soft, and the sheen of it had caught the light, making her chest ache. She'd punished herself by not taking it out of the dustcover for a few days, and then told herself not to be so stupid, that she had to try it on to see if it fitted. And of course it did. Like a glove. It flattered her, too, and the teenager she'd once been, who'd been so envious of her sister, had gloried in its beauty, feeling like a princess.

She hadn't indulged that, putting the gown away until the day of the gala had come around, and she'd told herself she was forcing herself to wear it. That she didn't like it and she'd tell him so too, so he knew he shouldn't buy her anything else.

Then, of course, he'd looked so devastatingly handsome, and had first of all unsettled her by telling her how stunning she looked, then by somehow seeing that, no matter what she told herself, she *did* like the dress and didn't want to admit it.

God, he was so annoyingly perceptive. She shouldn't have told him all those details about Chrissy, but she'd wanted him to stop asking questions and shock him into silence. But if he'd been shocked, he hadn't shown it. He'd only told her that he wasn't like Simon in any way. She hadn't wanted to believe him, but there had been nothing but truth in his blue gaze. He might be a notorious playboy, but he hadn't done any of the things that Simon had done to Chrissy, and something inside her was telling her that he wouldn't either.

He *wasn't* Simon, as he'd said, and she wasn't Chrissy, and whatever was between them, it didn't mean she'd end up going the same way as her sister. She had to stop snapping at him too, no matter how much he got under her skin. And he *was* getting under her skin—she could admit that now. Sitting next to her with that intense blue gaze on hers, the full force of his charisma directed at her. Everything about him unsettled her, including her own response to him.

Because she could feel it even now, after a week of trying to forget that kiss. All she had to do was look at him to feel his beautiful mouth on hers, the hard length of his body pressed against her curves, and the relentless, driving ache between her thighs that left her restless at night.

You're not the only one, though, remember? He feels it too.

He'd told her if she didn't stop looking at him she'd end up flat on her back with him inside her.

So she wasn't sure why she'd mentioned the kiss again—not when she knew what a Pandora's box that would open up. Then again, he was the one who'd mentioned having to touch one another, which he wasn't wrong about, since they were pretending they were in love.

You wanted to shake him, though. Don't lie. Like you did on the terrace.

Sadly, that was true. Yet she shouldn't give in to the temptation to do so, especially when she knew what had happened last time. Still, they weren't alone in his penthouse now. They were in a limo on the way to an event. So what did it matter if she pushed him just a little? Men used sex to manipulate women all the time, so why shouldn't she give him a taste of his own medicine?

'No, kissing you won't be a problem.' She raised a

brow in deliberate imitation of him. 'Did you think it would be?'

A blue flame ignited in his eyes. 'Well, you barely held yourself back from ravishing me on the terrace last week,' he murmured, his voice low and velvety. 'And *that* would not be appropriate at a gala fundraiser for child poverty.'

He might be rich and powerful, but he wants you. You could use that.

No, she wouldn't use that. Chrissy had used the power of her beauty, her sexuality, to earn herself the money she'd craved, and it had ended up backfiring on her. She'd become the one being used instead of vice versa. Yet another mistake Andie wasn't going to make.

'Are you ever serious about anything?' she snapped, forgetting that she wasn't supposed to snap at him for a moment. 'Not everything is a joke.'

Something shifted in his gaze, though she couldn't tell what it was. 'Of course it is, little siren. Life itself is just one big joke. Didn't you know that?'

'Why? Has everything in your life been so easy that child poverty is funny to you? Is that what it is?'

The flame in his eyes glittered. 'Easy...' he murmured, as if tasting the word. 'Everything in my life has been easy? Interesting word, that.'

'Of course it's been easy for you,' she said heedlessly. 'You're rich, powerful. You're drowning in privilege and you're—'

'My parents and my grandfather were killed in a car accident when I was twelve,' he interrupted flatly. 'My brother and I were in the car when it happened and we barely made it out alive. So, yes, you might very well say I'm drowning in privilege. The Teras family isn't exactly without means. But nothing about my life has been *easy*.'

She knew that about his family of course—most people did. But that he'd lost his parents at such a terrible age had only been a fact to her. Something she'd read in a bio. Not an actual event that had happened to a young boy. Yet it had. She could see the shadows of it in his blue eyes, and in the sudden burning anger beneath it.

Instantly, she felt awful. 'I didn't mean—'

'Then what *did* you mean? Perhaps you'd also like to know the details about the friend of my father who—' He broke off suddenly and, much to her surprise, looked away. 'What does it matter? You see what you want to see. Anyway, yes, life is one big joke. That's why Hydra Shipping donates to charities and why I attend so many fundraising galas. Because it's amusing to me, that's all.'

She stared at the pure line of his profile, seeing the tension in his jaw and shoulders. His voice had lost its harshness, but there was no warmth or amusement in it, no matter what he said about jokes, and for some reason she felt chastened.

She'd judged him, and harshly, and while part of her felt defensive about it, another kept whispering that maybe she'd been unfair. That he might be many things, but she couldn't keep sniping at him just because she was attracted to him and didn't like it.

He has lost people too, don't forget.

His parents and his grandfather. And she knew what it was like to lose a family member. The pain never left you.

Impulsively, she reached out and touched his thigh. 'I'm sorry,' she said. 'I'm too quick to judge sometimes.'

He went very still. 'Are you, indeed? I never would have guessed.'

Had she hurt him? She'd definitely offended him. Which shouldn't matter to her, because offending the privileged and shocking them was part of what she'd set out to do after Chrissy had died. But she didn't like the thought that she'd hurt him.

'I shouldn't be, I know,' she said, forcing herself to hold his gaze. 'I just…don't trust men in general. And so far I haven't met any who've made me change my mind.'

'Don't go pinning your hopes on me, little siren. I'm no better than the rest.'

Except she couldn't help thinking back to when he'd called her up to his office the day they'd met, when she'd only been wearing body paint. He'd put his jacket around her and hadn't looked at her body. Plenty of other men would have, and they wouldn't have cared if she'd noticed. But he hadn't. And when she'd kissed him, instead of taking advantage of her, he'd been the one to stop it, to warn her that it wasn't a good idea.

'Maybe not,' she said. 'But you're certainly not any worse—and, believe me, I've seen the worst.'

He stared at her, that flame still flickering in his gaze. 'I am sorry about your sister, Andromeda,' he said abruptly. 'Losing someone you love is very painful.'

For half a second a moment of understanding flowed between them, a shared acknowledgment of loss that eased something tight inside her. Then she became aware that her fingertips were still resting on his thigh, and beneath the expensive wool of his trousers she could feel the hard muscle and power of him. He was very warm. She was filled with the urge to slide her hand across that hard thigh of his and touch that other, very male part of him. To feel if he was as hard there as he was everywhere else.

His gaze gleamed brighter, as if he knew exactly what she was thinking. 'Yes,' he murmured. 'You can touch me. I won't bite.'

Insanity, of course. Utter madness. She should take her hand away immediately. Except…she couldn't quite bring herself to.

Then, when he gently picked up her hand and moved it to where she wanted it to be, so that her palm was pressed against his fly, she kept it there. And he *was* hard beneath her hand…so very, *very* hard…and he watched her, his blue gaze full of flames.

What would it be like to burn with him?

'We are here, Mr Teras,' the driver said.

Heat flooded through her as she realised that the limo had stopped and there were cameras going off outside. The driver was looking in his rear-view mirror and she still had her hand over Poseidon Teras's fly.

Andie made to pull her hand away, but he simply shifted her palm off him without fuss, as if it had been some innocuous touch and not her feeling how badly he wanted her.

'Well, little siren?' His gaze glittered in the lights coming through the window. 'Are you ready to show the world how in love with me you are?'

CHAPTER SIX

POSEIDON WAS FAIRLY sure Andromeda Lane was going to kill him at some point, and he had no one to blame but himself. He was the one who'd looked into her eyes and known exactly what she wanted—because he knew when a woman wanted him. So he'd told her that she could touch him. And when she'd blushed fiercely, he'd taken her hand and put it where they'd both wanted it to be.

She hadn't pulled away. She'd kept her palm there, resting lightly, a warm pressure that had made it almost impossible for him to breathe.

He shouldn't have done it. It had been a temptation too far. Yet he'd been caught in the moment, tangled up in the want and the heat he'd seen in her eyes.

Now he was going to have to get out of this limo with a hard-on in full view of the press. Not that he hadn't done such things before, though it was usually in the context of a night out at a nightclub or a celebrity party, rather than a gala fundraiser for children. Then again, maybe it wouldn't be the end of the world if people noticed. They'd assume certain things about Andromeda and his feelings for her, which would all work in nicely for their little game of pretence.

Your physical reaction to her isn't pretence.

Oh, *that* wasn't. He wanted her. He'd wanted her from the moment he'd first seen her, wearing nothing but body paint and holding a megaphone. That had been a purely physical attraction, it was true, yet now he was starting to find other things about her attractive as well—things that weren't to do with her beauty. Which was dangerous.

For example, not only was she beautiful and fierce, with a passionate heart, she'd also been quick to apologise when he'd let her judgement matter a little too much for comfort. He shouldn't have let it get under his skin in the first place, of course, but her assumptions about him had a hit a nerve he hadn't realised was there.

And she'd been apologetic. He might not have deserved the apology—she'd been right, despite his losing his parents so young, his background had been pretty privileged—but the fact that she'd given it without any prompting had eased some of his own temper.

Then there had been that moment when he'd offered his genuine sympathies for her sister's death, and they'd shared a few seconds of connection, a mutual understanding of grief.

He hadn't meant for that to happen. He hadn't meant to nearly give away the existence of Michel either, even though he hadn't thought of it for years and shouldn't be thinking about it now.

It had been good at first. An old friend of his father's,

Michel had been more than willing to give Poseidon the help he'd needed when he'd taken over Hydra Shipping, filling the void left by Poseidon's father's death. Until Michel had made it clear that in return for his support Poseidon needed to give him other things…such as his body, for example.

Poseidon had been young, desperate for Michel's support and approval, and so he'd given Michel what he'd asked for. And once Michel had taken it, he'd cut off all contact.

Poseidon had never heard from him again.

Poseidon had felt used after that, and stupid for letting it happen. Stupid for letting his grief over his father make him so open to manipulation. Stupid for letting Michel's betrayal be such a big deal.

Stupid for caring.

So, that had been the end of caring. For good.

He never thought of it these days. He'd dismissed it from his mind as a youthful mistake, now long forgotten. And he didn't know why he'd almost told Andromeda when he'd never told anyone else—not even Asterion. It certainly hadn't been on a par with losing his parents in terms of trauma, so it shouldn't have even crossed his mind. The only mercy was that he'd stopped himself before he'd said anything else.

Cameras flashed as he got out of the limo and then turned to help Andromeda. The flush that had washed through her lovely face as he'd put her hand on him was still there, and when her gaze met his she went even pinker.

The blood hammered in his veins, a rushing pulse of desire, but they were in full view of the press, so all he did was offer his arm, and she took it, smiling for the cameras as they went up the stairs together.

He couldn't stop looking at her. The cameras kept flashing, and people called his name, but he ignored them. She was so beautiful in that gown, and even though the smiles she gave were fake, they lit her face like sunlight. It made him desperate to know what one of her real smiles would look like and whether he might ever be the cause. He wanted to be the cause.

At the top of the stairs he slid an arm around her waist and pulled her in close—because he could. Because they were supposed to be pretending to be in love and he was going to take full advantage of being close to her while he could.

She stiffened and then, as if she'd remembered what they were supposed to do, relaxed, allowing his arm to settle around her. He put a possessive hand on her hip, feeling the warmth of her body beneath the thin silk of her gown. It was intoxicating.

That is not going to make things easier.

No, but he could handle himself. Nothing would happen. But Dimitra was sharp-eyed and wise to his ways, so it had to look believable.

The Hintze Hall, where the gala was being held, looked magnificent. The dramatic Romanesque arches lining it were lit up in blue and pink, as was the huge skeleton of a blue whale that hung suspended in the air above the hall itself. There was a dramatic central staircase that looked like a cascade of flowers, and more tubs of flowers and trees dotted here and there.

Delicate music floated in the air, along with the buzz of conversation, while wait staff in formal black and white threaded through the bejewelled crowd with trays of expensive French champagne.

Andromeda's eyes were wide and her mouth was open slightly, as if she'd never seen anything like it in her entire life. It was such a different expression from her normal look of distrust, suspicion, and challenge that he almost stopped dead in his tracks.

She should look at you like that.

Like her smiles. They should be for him too.

The air had gone out of him and he couldn't understand why. She was just a woman, and no different from any other, yet he hadn't been obsessed with another woman's smiles the way he was with hers. And he'd never wanted another woman to look at him with that same intriguing combination of awe and wonder. But all the lack of understanding in the world didn't change the intensity of the desire inside him.

She should look at him like that in bed, with her wide green eyes gazing up into his, awestruck at the pleasure he was giving her...

The thought stuck in his head like a splinter and he couldn't get it out. He'd slip those silky straps from her pale shoulders and the silk would fall slowly down, revealing her full breasts. She wasn't wearing a bra and they would—

Someone said his name and he forced himself back to

reality, reluctantly tearing his gaze from Andromeda's face as people greeted him.

It was a struggle, but he managed it, introducing her around and purposely singling out the people he thought she and her addiction service would find useful—because, after all, that was what he'd promised her. It was interesting to watch her speak to them. She was friendly and warm, almost the opposite of the shouting termagant she'd been outside his office that day, and he wanted that warmth of hers too. He wanted it directed at him. He'd had a taste of it in the limo earlier, in that moment of shared understanding, and he wanted more.

'Why do you keep staring at me?' she murmured, as they finished chatting with one group of people and Poseidon steered her in the direction of another.

'Because I didn't know you even knew what a smile was.' His hand was on her hip again, as if her curves had been made to fit in his palm, so he kept it there.

'I feel that's getting perilously close to saying *You should smile more.*'

Amusement curled through him. 'I would never say that, little siren. If anything, I think you should smile less. You're even more magnificent when you're angry.'

She gave him a sidelong glance, which amused him still further, but then they reached the group he was aiming for and the round of introductions began again.

He couldn't still the beat of his heart. Couldn't slow the pounding rush of blood in his veins. She was so close to him, her sweet vanilla scent all around him, the warmth of her skin against his, and he couldn't concentrate on a single thing. It was maddening.

He'd always thought that he was in perfect control of himself, but ever since that kiss that control had felt as if it was slipping through his fingers, and he knew there was only one answer for it. He either put some distance between them or—

Took her to bed?

No. He'd told himself sex was off the table and he wasn't changing his mind. Yet he couldn't do distance either—not with the game of pretence they were playing. Which meant he was going to have to get himself in hand if he was to survive the night.

Eventually, about an hour and a half after they'd arrived, his control in tatters, Poseidon guided her to an empty couch positioned behind some tubs of flowers. 'Sit,' he said, gesturing to the couch. 'I'll go and get you a drink.' And get himself a well-earned break from the constant pull of need she'd set up inside him.

She glanced at the couch, and as she did so he became aware that one of the photographers for the evening had his camera pointed in their direction. *Damn.* A picture of her standing alone in the hall wasn't exactly what they'd been going for, so he pulled her in close instead.

'There's a photographer not far away and he's looking in our direction,' he murmured in her ear. 'We should take advantage of it.'

Her cheeks were flushed, her eyes darkening as she glanced up at him. 'So, I should look at you like this?'

'Yes. Just like that.'

He felt caught by that gaze of hers, held hostage by it, and he found himself lifting a hand and cupping her cheek the way he had done that day on the terrace of his penthouse. Her skin was warm beneath his palm and felt like silk, and she didn't move.

'Lean into my hand, little siren,' he said quietly. 'Look at me as if you want to devour me whole.'

She didn't hesitate, leaning into his palm as he'd instructed, her gaze darkening still further. 'Are you going to kiss me?'

Her voice was low and husky and she didn't sound at all upset by that.

'Yes.' He didn't think he'd be able *not* to. 'The opportunity is too good to miss, no?'

This is a mistake.

It wasn't. As he'd said, this was the perfect opportunity to leave no doubt in the public's mind about the nature of their relationship. A shared secret kiss at a gala.

But you want it too much.

He ignored the thought, lowering his head instead and brushing his mouth lightly over hers. At least, that was what it was supposed to be—a moment of light contact, a brief opportunity for the photographer to get a picture.

Yet as soon as their lips touched it felt as if the air around them had ignited, heat exploding like petrol thrown over an open fire.

She made a sighing sound, her hands pressing against his chest, her mouth opening beneath his like a flower, so sweet, and he was utterly unable to stop himself from taking advantage. He swept his tongue into her mouth, deepening the kiss, tasting her, exploring her, and her head went back allowing him greater access. He slid his fingers into her hair and curled them into the soft silken mass, suddenly ravenous for her in a way he'd never experienced with anyone before.

You can't get this desperate.

The thought was loud in his head before becoming lost under a wave of desire as she pressed herself against him, leaning into him as if she was as desperate to be as close to him as he was to her.

He slid his other hand from her hip to curve over her rear, cupping her, urging her hips against his, so he could press his hard, aching shaft against the softness and heat between her thighs. She felt unbelievably good, and she smelled of sweet musk and vanilla. Good God, he wanted to eat her alive.

He kissed her deeper, hotter, oblivious to the fact that the hall was full of people and he'd only meant the initial kiss to be pretend. There was nothing pretend about this kiss. He felt hungry, demanding. He wanted to push her up against a wall somewhere, haul her gown up, slide his hand between her thighs and stroke the softness there, then bury himself inside her and satisfy this insatiable hunger once and for all.

And why not? Perhaps the reason for this desperation was because he'd been denying himself. Perhaps if he stopped, if he allowed himself to have what he wanted, then it would burn itself out.

He squeezed her rear gently, feeling her shiver and

arch against him, and somewhere a camera flashed, bringing him back to reality.

Forcing himself to let go of her hair, he lifted his head and looked down into the endless green darkness of her eyes. There was heat there, and desperation, and hunger. The same hunger he felt.

'I want you,' he said starkly, unable to be anything but blatantly honest. 'I want you now. Here.'

She was trembling, her breathing fast and hard. 'Yes,' she whispered, her gaze dropping to his mouth. 'Yes. Please.'

He couldn't think. Part of him was trying to remind him that he wasn't supposed to be touching her, that this was wrong—but, as he'd already thought, perhaps it was the denial that was wrong. Perhaps the only way out of this was to satisfy the hunger, get rid of this desperation once and for all.

He stepped away from her, then took her hand. 'Come with me,' he said.

Andie's heart was beating far too hard and far too fast, and the ache between her thighs was a steady pressure that she knew only one thing would ease.

Him.

She knew it wasn't a good idea. In fact, it was the last thing she should want, and especially with him. But ever since she'd laid her hand on him in the limo she hadn't been able to think of anything else.

Sex was something she'd avoided so far, and deliberately. Chrissy had ruined herself over it and Andie never wanted to allow a man that much power over her. So far, she hadn't regretted her decision, but now… Now she couldn't help wondering if that had been a bad idea. Because maybe if she'd had a relationship, or even a one-night stand, then she wouldn't now be so at the mercy of her own body's demands.

Poseidon had had his arm around her all evening, his large palm resting on her hip, his warmth soaking through the fine silk of her gown. She'd been so insanely aware of both that hand and his body next to hers she'd barely been able to concentrate on anything else. She'd smiled at people, shaken their hands, had conversations of some kind, but she couldn't remember what they'd talked about or recall their names.

The only thing that felt real in this whole dream of an evening was him. Strange, when wearing a beautiful gown at a star-studded gala should have been a high point in her life, giving her, as it did, a taste of what her sister had had.

Then he'd kissed her. She shouldn't have agreed to it—she should have pushed him away after that first second of contact. Yet she hadn't. No, she'd stepped in even closer, opened her mouth beneath his and let him kiss her. Let his rich flavour turn her inside out. Let herself get dizzy with his scent, and the heat of his body, and the hard evidence of his desire pressing between her thighs.

She might have refused if he hadn't told her that he wanted her in that voice raw with need. As if he was desperate. As if she'd pushed him, a notorious playboy, to the end of his control.

Taking his hand and letting him lead her out of the hall was the height of stupidity, but she didn't pull away. Because she wanted him too, as desperately as he wanted her. And she also wanted to know the nature of the thing that had led Chrissy down the path to ruin. Some part of her needed to know, to experience it for herself, to understand.

So she followed him into a short, darkened hallway not far from the hall's main entrance. And when he pulled her into it, and pushed her up against the wall, she didn't protest.

His blue gaze was all fire as he put his hands on the wall on either side of her head, caging her against it.

'Can you be quiet?' he asked. 'Very, *very* quiet?'

Her whole body trembled with anticipation and need. 'Yes,' she said breathlessly, and then she added, because it was only fair that he should know, 'I… I haven't done this before.'

He frowned. 'What do you mean? Had sex in a public place?'

Perhaps she shouldn't have said anything. Then again, it was too late now. 'No. Sex, full stop.'

Shock flared in his eyes and he stiffened. 'Oh, Andromeda…'

But she didn't want him to pull away, so she reached for him, sliding her hands up and over the hard wall of his chest.

'Show me,' she whispered. 'I want to know why my

sister followed a man who ruined her. I want to know what's so great about sex that people destroy themselves for it.'

He let out a breath. 'It shouldn't be like this…not your first time.'

'Why not?' She looked up into the vivid blue of his eyes, seeing the flames still blazing bright in them. 'Shouldn't I be the one to choose when and where?'

'It's true. You should.'

He lifted a hand and pushed a curl behind her ear, his fingertips brushing her skin and making her shiver. Then his fingers dropped to the strap of her gown on her left shoulder.

'In which case, tell me if you want me to stop.'

Slowly, he eased the strap down, keeping his gaze on hers, and she felt the fabric fall, leaving her breast bare.

She shivered, her skin tight and hot, and when he looked down she shivered again.

'So beautiful,' he breathed, tracing the delicate curve of her breast with light fingertips, before brushing them lightly across her nipple.

His touch was electric, a sharp jolt of sensation that made her gasp and arch her back against the wall, and the sound echoed softly around them.

'Hush,' Poseidon murmured, his wicked fingertips continuing to caress her sensitive breast. 'There are people in the hallway.'

She could hear them, too…the buzz of light chatter and the sound of laughter. So close. They could be found at any moment. That should have made her embarrassed, but it didn't. If anything, the thought of discovery only added to the wild excitement coursing through her, making her heart beat hard and the pulsing ache between her thighs get worse.

'Please,' she whispered, her fingers curling into his shirt to bring him closer. 'Poseidon...'

He leaned in, giving her what she wanted, which was his mouth on hers, kissing her deeply, and with so much heat she thought she might actually catch on fire. Then his hand was smoothing down her hip to her thigh, fingers curling in the silk of her gown and lifting it.

This is a mistake. Are you really going to let him take you up against a wall at a gala?

The thought spun through her fevered brain for a moment, then disappeared as quickly as it had come. She didn't care. She'd never wanted anything as badly as she wanted him right now. So she didn't stop him as he lifted her gown and slid his hand between her thighs, his fingers slipping beneath the damp fabric of her knickers and stroking her. She was aching, and slick, and, when he touched her the pleasure was so intense she had to bite her lip hard to stop from crying out.

'No,' he whispered. 'Give me your cries, little siren. Scream if you need to.' Then he bent and kissed her, his fingers exploring her, stroking her soft, wet flesh, then sliding wickedly inside her.

She moaned into his mouth as the aching pressure built and built—and then he did something with his fingers that released it in a burst of wild pleasure that had her crying out against his lips and writhing in his arms.

He leaned in, pressing her body harder against the wall, containing her with his warmth and strength as the pleasure cascaded through her, making her shake and shake. After the trembles had eased, he got out his wallet and extracted a condom, dealing with the issue of protection swiftly and with minimal fuss. Then he slid one hand behind her knee and lifted her leg up, hooking it around his hip.

His eyes were blazing blue and she stared up into them, her whole body drawn tight with anticipation. Then he was pressing forward, pushing inside her, gently and slowly, and she could feel herself stretching around him in the most exquisite way. It was supposed to be painful—that was what Chrissy had told her—but she didn't feel any pain, only a sense of wonder.

She'd never thought she'd want a man to get so close, to allow him into her body, yet it was different with Poseidon. He wasn't just any man and he felt…amazing. There was so much intensity in his face as he looked at her, as if he felt the same wonder she did at this closeness, this intimacy. No one had ever looked at her that way…not one single person.

'Poseidon,' she whispered, simply for the sheer pleasure of saying his name.

He murmured something raw in what she thought must be Greek, and then he lifted her leg a bit higher, sliding even deeper, making a connection so intimate it took her breath away. He didn't move—not immediately—and the two of them pressed together.

She was amazed at the beauty of him like this. There was no artifice to him now, no dryly amused playboy. Only a man looking at her with such hunger and such passion. He hid it well, but she could see it now, laid bare before her. He'd lied when he'd said he didn't care about anything, that life was just a big joke, because how could a man who burned this intensely not care? How could he not feel when all evidence to the contrary blazed so brightly in his eyes?

He began to move, slowly at first, his hips setting a rhythm that had her shaking. Her hands were gripping his shoulders, her nails digging into his jacket, as the pleasure began to coil tighter and tighter, breaking her open, breaking her apart.

'Andromeda,' he said in a low, ragged voice. *'Asteri mou.'*

He began to move faster, his gaze holding hers, and she felt as if she was falling into the endless blue of his eyes. Into the endless pleasure of him inside her. The driving thrust of his hips and the heat of his hard body moving against her.

The pleasure became frantic, and she was desperate, the effort not to cry out almost too much for her. As if he knew exactly what she needed, he bent again and covered her mouth, at the same time slipping a hand between her thighs, to where they were joined. He stroked her once, twice. Then that aching pressure inside her sprang apart, exploding in a wild shower of sparks. Pleasure expanded inside her, and she screamed into his mouth as it took her.

Then it was his turn, his rhythm hard and fast, until he turned his face into her hair and climax took him as well.

For a long moment all she could do was stand there, pressed against his heat, listening to the sounds of people talking in the hallway, the echoes of pleasure still crashing inside her.

She was aware, too, that a part of her was growing a little panicky. Because Chrissy had been very clear about men, and what they expected, and how, after you'd given them what they wanted, you were disposable.

Ridiculous to panic—because why did she care if Poseidon pushed himself away from her and never spoke to her again? No, of course she didn't. If anything, *she* had been the one to take what she wanted from *him*, and now she'd had it, what did she even need him for?

She readied herself to push him away, before he could do the same to her, only to be shocked when abruptly his hand cupped her cheek, lifting her face so he could look in her eyes.

'Are you okay?' he asked, his gaze searching. 'Did I hurt you?'

A strange lump of emotion sat in her throat and she wasn't sure where it had come from. It made her feel raw and vulnerable, and she didn't like it.

'No,' she forced out, trying to sound casual. 'I'm fine.'

Yet the look in his eyes intensified, and his thumb

passed over her cheekbone in a gentle caress. 'Come home with me. I want you in my bed.'

She swallowed, her mouth dry. This was not what Chrissy had said about men. Once they'd had what they wanted from you they discarded you—that was what she'd said. Unless they were Simon, of course. Then again, Simon had wanted other things from Chrissy.

Poseidon's fingers gripped her chin, and the look in his eyes turned even hotter. 'I only want a night, little siren,' he said, low and insistent. 'That's all. You've been killing me for a week now, and five minutes up against a wall isn't going to cut it.'

The honesty in his voice and the intensity in his eyes echoed inside her, striking a chord in her soul. He wanted her. He *wanted* her. The girl who hadn't been able to save her sister. He wanted her very badly indeed.

'I thought we weren't going to do this,' she said.

'We weren't. But give me one night, Andromeda. Just one.'

'Why? Why me?'

He was silent a moment, but his gaze was devouring. 'I'd love to say it's only chemistry, but… You're the most passionate woman I've ever met and I want a night when all that passion is mine.'

Again, his honesty left her speechless, almost stripped bare. She hadn't expected that from him, and it made her want to be equally honest back.

But you have to be careful. You don't want to end up like Chrissy.

She wouldn't. She knew the dangers, and it would

be only one night and no more. What harm could it do? Once she'd had that night, and fully explored what it was that had addicted her sister, she'd walk away. It would be a good test for herself.

'Yes,' she said, giving up on her resistance and leaning into the heat of his body. 'I want that too. Take me home, Poseidon.'

CHAPTER SEVEN

THE CHANDELIERS OF La Salle de Europe in the Casino de Monte Carlo lit up the opulent gilt ceiling and the frescos on the gilt-covered walls, before glittering off the jewels of the couture-clad crowd milling below.

The room was full of the buzz of conversation and the clatter of the roulette wheel, croupiers calling, and cheers coming from those gathered to play at the tables.

Poseidon, leaning against the wall near one of the blackjack tables, surveyed his party with some satisfaction, before glancing at the woman standing next to him.

Tonight, Andromeda wore a Grecian gown of pale gold silk—another dress he'd taken great pleasure in picking especially for her. As he'd thought, the colour complemented her skin and brought out the fire in her red-gold curls. She wore her hair piled on top of her head, with a few artful ringlets allowed to dangle here and there, and she looked like the goddess she was.

Fierce need gripped him, the way it had been gripping him the whole two weeks since their one night together, at the most inopportune times.

He couldn't stop thinking about it. About her and

what a revelation she'd been. Fire in his hands, just as he'd thought. Passionate, hungry, curious too. And he'd known the second he'd kissed her goodbye the next morning that one night wasn't going to be enough.

Not nearly enough.

He wanted more.

Perhaps he shouldn't have taken her the way he had, the night of their first public appearance, in a dark hallway up against a wall, with people nearby. Especially considering she'd been a virgin. But he'd wanted her too much to stop. He'd appreciated her telling him, though, just as he'd appreciated her telling him that she was very sure she wanted him and that she was the one who should get to choose where her first time was.

Choice was important to him, for very good reasons.

But, whether it was wrong or not, he hadn't regretted it. Watching her green eyes widen with shocked pleasure as he'd pushed inside her had been a glory, as had feeling the slick heat of her sex grip him tight. And when he'd kissed her, taking her cries of ecstasy into his mouth as she'd climaxed, he'd been so pushed to the edge of his control he'd barely been able to hold on.

It had never been like that for him. *Never*.

He had to have another night.

Of course, he shouldn't want more. One night, they'd agreed, just one. But denial only made the fire burn hotter, and the most logical thing was to feed it until there was nothing left to burn.

So the following day, after she'd gone, he'd decided their next public appearance would be something special, that he'd pull out all the stops. He thought she might want another night too, but he didn't want to assume and so wouldn't leave anything to chance.

He was going to seduce her, and thoroughly, and to do that he was going to organise his own event. An event especially for her, which would incorporate Chrissy's Hope and yet more donations. The cause was worthy, naturally, but his main focus would be on pleasing Andromeda.

It was very short notice to organise such an event, but his PR team were excellent and he had a couple of contacts in Monte Carlo who owed him a favour or two. As for getting enough guests, there was no one in the rich, moneyed, and powerful circles he moved in who'd refuse one of his invitations—especially if it involved a party for a good cause. A party such as an exclusive fundraising night at a luxury casino in Monte Carlo with all the winnings going to Chrissy's Hope.

Andromeda had been wary at first, when he'd called her to discuss it, and had pointed out to him that perhaps having a gambling event to raise funds for an addiction service would be sending out mixed messages. Which was fair. But he'd countered with the idea that rich people liked to gamble and, if it involved an exclusive party, free alcohol, celebrity guests, plus all the money going to a good cause, not only would they come in droves, they'd also probably end up giving more as a sop to their conscience.

Cynical of him, as she'd said, but also true.

He'd thought she might protest at the gown, or at the

very least insist on staying somewhere downmarket and not the luxury hotel he had them booked at—separate rooms, of course, since he wasn't assuming—yet she hadn't.

She *had* declined a seat on his private jet, telling him she had some other business to attend to first and would join him in Monaco in time for the event. He'd paid for her flights, though she insisted on economy and he hadn't argued. If she wanted to travel in discomfort that was her choice.

He'd told her to meet him in the lobby of their hotel, so they could travel to the event together, and when she had, resplendent in that gown, all the breath had left his body. She'd looked exquisite. And she'd smiled at him, as if she was as pleased to see him as he was to see her, and it had been as if his whole world had slowed down and stopped.

It was still stopped now.

She was gazing out over the crowd, a glass of champagne in her hand, her pretty face still flushed with excitement. They'd just come from the roulette table, where he'd showed her how to play, and she'd ended up winning a large amount of money for Chrissy's Hope. She might not want to admit it, but she'd enjoyed the game as much as she had the winning, he was sure. In fact, he was beginning to suspect that she liked games rather more than she was letting on.

'Are you having a good time?' he asked, watching her face.

She glanced at him, her green eyes alight. 'Yes. I

know I was dubious about this, but it's a lot more fun than I thought it would be. And all the money is going to Chrissy's Hope…' Another of her beautiful smiles curved her mouth. 'Thank you, Poseidon.'

A feeling he didn't recognise shifted in his chest…a kind of tightness. But then a couple of photographers passed by, taking pictures, so he ignored the sensation, reaching for her and pulling her in close. Only to feel her go rigid in his arms.

He glanced down at her in concern, but she wasn't looking at him. Her gaze was on the crowd by the blackjack table. Her face had gone white, her smile vanishing.

The tightness in his chest tightened still further. 'What is it?' he asked. 'You've gone pale.'

She looked down at the glass in her hand. 'Nothing.'

'It's not nothing, Andromeda. You look like you've seen a ghost.'

She shook her head, but he drew her closer and at the same time turned them both slightly, shielding her with his body from the rest of the room and the photographers.

'Tell me,' he murmured quietly. 'You look upset.'

She was silent a moment, then she glanced up at him. 'Why did you do this? The party, I mean? You must have had a hundred other events we could have gone to. You didn't have to organise one especially for me.'

This wasn't what was bothering her, he was certain. She'd seen something, or maybe someone, who'd upset her. But if she didn't want to tell him he wouldn't push.

'I thought you were enjoying yourself,' he pointed out mildly.

'I am, but… You've already agreed to sponsor Chrissy's Hope in return for me marrying you.' She gestured to the room. 'You didn't need to do all this as well.'

'I didn't, it's true.' He settled her more firmly against him. 'But I can't lie and say I don't have any ulterior motives.'

She regained a bit of colour, which was good, and a flash of her fiery spirit was showing in her eyes. 'Of course you have ulterior motives. I presume you're going to share them with me?'

He gazed down at her, very conscious of what her proximity was doing to him. Her warmth and sweet scent were making him hard, and all he could think about was taking her back to their hotel and getting rid of that gown, sating himself on her beautiful body again. It had been two weeks since he'd touched her and, right now, every second of those weeks were weighing on him.

Abruptly, he was tired of his own games. 'My ulterior motive is you,' he said bluntly. 'I want another night, Andromeda.'

More colour flushed her cheeks, pink and pretty. 'So all of this is…what? To get me into bed again?'

He lifted a brow. 'Is it too much?'

She gazed at him for a second, then her mouth softened and curved slightly. 'You could have just asked me, you know. You didn't need to make it an entire production.'

A savage kick of satisfaction caught at him. So, she

did want more. He'd known she would. 'You don't think you're worth an entire production, little siren?'

She let out a breath. 'But you've gone to so much trouble.'

'You like a pretty dress and a glitzy event.' He smoothed his hand over her hips. 'And don't bother denying it. I know you do.'

'Poseidon…'

'It's okay to enjoy it, Andromeda,' he said, a bit more insistently. 'It doesn't mean you're going to suddenly turn into your sister.'

Because of course that was what she was worried about, wasn't it?

She opened her mouth, probably to protest, but he held up a hand.

'So,' he went on, 'you should relax and enjoy yourself, because it's for a good cause. Plus, it's going to look even better for our little bit of relationship theatre, don't you think? Me doing something thoughtful for my beautiful new girlfriend.'

An expression flickered over her face that he couldn't read, but then finally the tension left her and she gave him another one of her beautiful smiles.

'I suppose when you put it like that, I can't really refuse.'

Another surge of satisfaction filled him. 'I hope that means *Yes, Poseidon, I'd love to have another night with you.*'

Her smile turned into something that was a little

wicked, yet also shy at the same time, and it made the desire inside him burn even hotter.

'You said only one night,' she murmured.

'I did,' he agreed. 'But you were such a glory, little siren, that I can't resist another. Would that really be so bad?'

She lifted her champagne and took a slow, meditative sip, staring at him over the rim of her glass. 'No,' she said at last. 'No, it really wouldn't.'

'In that case, let's—'

'Excuse me,' a voice interrupted from behind him. 'Andie? Is that you?'

Poseidon saw the moment the colour left Andromeda's face again, fury igniting in her green eyes.

'Simon,' she said flatly. 'What the hell are you doing here?'

Andie fought to get a handle on her fury and shock. She'd thought she'd seen Simon in the crowd near the blackjack table just before, but had convinced herself that she was seeing things. He'd pretty much vanished after Chrissy had died—he hadn't even come to the funeral—and she'd been too angry to keep track of him. Yes, he was rich and well-connected, and he liked a party, but he surely couldn't be *here*.

Then again, he must have links to Poseidon since he'd been the one to take Chrissy to the party on that yacht. Poseidon's yacht.

He was standing behind Poseidon, all smooth and handsome in his tux, smiling the smile that Andie had once thought so dreamy. He'd dazzled her once, the way he'd dazzled Chrissy, but now, looking at him, she couldn't understand what she'd seen in him.

His smile was more of a smirk than anything sexy, and he'd used too much hair product, making his hair look oily instead of glossy. There were creases in his tux jacket, and lines of dissipation around his eyes and mouth. He looked…sleazy. A man who'd indulged himself far too much and far too often.

Anger was burning a hole in her chest, and the urge to scream at him, then throw her drink in his face for what he'd done to her sister, was almost overwhelming. But she couldn't do that here—not in this room full of people having fun and donating large sums of money for Chrissy's Hope.

Instead, much to her horror, she felt her eyes prick with ridiculous tears of fury.

Simon was smirking at her as if nothing was wrong. 'Wow, you look fantastic, sweetheart. I've been wondering how you were doing. You should join me for a—'

'She will not be going anywhere with you,' Poseidon said with utter finality, stepping in front of her as if to shield her. 'So you're Simon. You're the one who invited Chrissy to that party onboard *Thetis*. Andromeda tells me you're also the one who provided the drugs that night.'

Simon had gone white, making the blue eyes she'd always thought an amazing colour look washed out. 'Teras, right?' He gave Poseidon an ingratiating smile.

'Good to meet you at last. I'm Simon Winchester.' He held out a hand.

Poseidon ignored it, and it struck Andie, all at once, how different the two men were. On the surface, they were both rich and handsome—the same, almost. Yet one man was the most intrinsically selfish man she'd ever met, while the other was…protective. More caring that he'd ever admit. And kinder too.

Poseidon was a man who'd told her he didn't care about anything, and yet he cared enough about his grandmother that he was marrying a complete stranger without a word of protest, simply because she'd asked him to. He'd been up-front with her from the start about what he wanted, including all his ulterior motives, and he cared enough about her to respect her choices.

Simon respected no one's choices and didn't care about anyone but himself. And what she'd once thought of as charm had turned out to be only sleaze.

Now, looking at the two of them, she couldn't understand how she'd ever thought Poseidon was in any way, shape or form like Simon.

Poseidon had returned Simon's smile, but his was white and sharp and terrifying. 'Tell me, who let you into my party?'

Simon bristled. 'I was invited. A friend of mine—'

'I'm rescinding the invitation.' Poseidon lifted a finger and abruptly a number of security guards appeared. 'You can leave under your own steam or I'll have security carry you out.' His smile widened. 'And if you ever approach Andromeda again, including by phone or text or email, I'll have your hide.'

A little shock went down Andromeda's spine. He was protecting her, wasn't he? Defending her. Of course she didn't need defending, but rage was still twisting in her gut, along with a healthy amount of grief, and she didn't want to have a confrontation with Simon. Not here.

'Are you threatening me, Teras?' Simon blustered.

'Of course I'm threatening you, you idiot,' Poseidon said pleasantly. 'If you have a problem with it, feel free to take it up with the police. I'm sure they'll be very interested to hear about a few nasty little habits of yours.'

Simon started to say something else, but by that stage, clearly losing patience with him, Poseidon had lifted another finger and, with relatively little fuss, Simon was escorted from the casino by security guards.

Then Poseidon turned, slid a steadying hand beneath Andie's elbow. Somehow she found herself being ushered from the main gaming room and into another smaller but no less opulent room, with a lounge area, where there were mercifully no people.

'Are you all right?' he asked as he steered her towards one of the velvet-covered couches. 'If I'd known he was coming I would have had Security watch out for him at the door.'

Andie put her champagne glass down on the small table beside the couch and took a shaky breath. 'I'm okay. It was just a shock. I didn't expect him to turn up.'

'Was that why you went pale earlier?'

So he'd noticed that. Well, that wasn't a surprise. He noticed a lot of things about her.

'Yes.'

There wasn't any point in denying that, nor the echoes of grief that were now resounding inside her as her anger dissipated.

'I haven't seen him for years. Not since Chrissy died. He didn't come to her funeral…didn't send any form of condolences. Basically he vanished. I used to think he was so handsome.'

Her throat was tight. She hadn't told anyone any of this before, yet now the words kept on spilling out.

'I used to be so envious of Chrissy. Because she had this amazing guy interested in her, who showered her with gifts and all his attention. And she got to go to the most amazing parties, travel to wonderful places, have all these exciting experiences.'

She looked down at her hands twisted in her lap.

'Then I found out the truth. How Simon had been using her, giving her drugs and passing her around his friends.'

'I lied,' Poseidon said flatly. 'When I told him I'd get the police involved, that wasn't a threat. That was a promise.'

But a lead weight was sitting in the pit of Andie's stomach all of a sudden.

'He was only part of the problem. The real issue was that she thought she was in love with him and so she did everything he told her to do. I tried to tell her that maybe taking drugs in nightclubs wasn't a good idea, that maybe she should lay off going to parties every night, but…she didn't listen.'

Andie swallowed, grief constricting her throat.

'She told me that she was fine, that she was having a great time and that I was just jealous.'

Unexpectedly, Poseidon reached out and took her cold hands in his large ones, and she felt the shock of his touch echo through her entire body. His grip was so warm, easing the tension inside her.

'How old were you when Chrissy died?' Poseidon asked.

'Fifteen.'

His fingers around hers were so warm. 'And did you think you should have saved her?'

Andie closed her eyes.

You should have saved her. If you'd only tried harder.

'I tried talking to Mum about her,' she said hoarsely. 'But Mum wouldn't listen either. She thought Chrissy was doing well for herself and didn't need saving.'

'You did what you could.' He sounded so reasonable. 'Chrissy was older than you and she made her own choices. No, they weren't good ones, but you can't take responsibility for them. You can't take responsibility for anyone's choices—not as an adult, and certainly not at fifteen.'

She'd gone beyond trying to keep everything contained. Now she couldn't help but let it spill out—all the doubts and worries she'd had, all her fears.

'But I was the only one who could see the path she was heading down, Poseidon. No one else did. And no one else would listen.' Tears pricked at the backs of her eyes, but she refused to let them fall. 'I'm sure there was more I could have done, but I just…gave up in the end. I didn't know what else to do.'

He let her hands go then, and she found herself pulled into his arms. She didn't fight, though. Instead, an odd feeling of security filled her, as if there could be a hurricane or a tidal wave, but as long as he held her she'd remain safe. Anchored.

'You did what you could,' he said, with such certainty that she almost believed him. 'But you were only fifteen. You tried, Andromeda. That's all anyone can do. Chrissy's choices were her own and they're not yours to bear. The only control you have is over the ones you make yourself.'

He's right. And you have to accept that, because what's the alternative?

The alternative was to continually beat herself up for all the things she hadn't done.

'I suppose so,' she said at last.

Poseidon eased a curl behind her ear, his blue gaze intense. 'Is that why you deny yourself the things you enjoy? Is it really because you think you're too like Chrissy? Or are you just punishing yourself?'

He's right about that, too.

That vulnerable feeling crept through her again, making her want to turn away from him, but his fingers caught her chin before she could, holding her firmly.

'You loved your sister, *asteri mou*, and you did what you could for her. But you can't change what happened to her, so why keep going over it?' His blue eyes were full of concern. 'Stop torturing yourself, little siren. It doesn't do you any good. Let yourself enjoy life's pleasures while you can, hmm?'

And somehow the weight inside her eased, and the tightness in her chest was released. He was right. There *was* no point going over things she couldn't change. And, to a certain extent, punishing herself was exactly what she was doing.

Denying yourself him is part of the punishment.

That was true too. Though it wasn't only punishment—there was a certain amount of fear too. Because now she'd had a taste of what had led Chrissy to her doom. Now, finally, she understood the breathless grip of chemistry, the dizzying rush of pleasure. The intensity of their connection was addictive, so she'd tried to push the night she and Poseidon had had out of her mind, not go back over it again and again.

But she hadn't been able to. Memories of that night had continued to plague her. The feel of his hands on her, the taste of him, the unbelievable pleasure he'd given her. And it had been *so* much pleasure.

The depth of her need had frightened her, so while she'd allowed herself the dress, she'd denied herself the pleasure of being on his private jet, the pleasure of his company, delaying it as much as she could.

But then, at that overly lavish hotel, as she'd come into the lobby to meet him, breathless at the thought despite herself, he'd started towards her, magnificent in his black evening clothes, and her heart had leaped inside her chest. And her feminine awareness had been a pulse between her thighs, deep and strong.

She wished he wasn't right about her liking a glitzy event, but she did. It put distance between her and the council flat and the suffocating grief that had enveloped her after Chrissy had died and her mother retreating into depression. Here there were glittering lights and people laughing, wonderful clothes and fine champagne, and the most beautiful man at her side.

Chrissy would want you to have it. She'd approve.

Maybe she would…maybe she wouldn't. Either way, she wasn't here now. But Poseidon was. And he wasn't Simon. He'd never do the things Simon had done, and she wasn't Chrissy.

Taking what he was offering wasn't going to lead to her doom—and, besides, life was short. Why deny herself?

Andromeda lifted her hands, threading her fingers through the thick black silk of his hair. 'Another night,' she murmured. 'Let's take it now.'

And she drew his mouth down on hers.

CHAPTER EIGHT

THE LITTLE ISLAND kingdom glowed like a jewel in the middle of the deep blue of the sea as the plane came in to land. It was one of the world's prettiest airports, apparently, but Poseidon had never paid much attention to its beauty—not when every time he landed dread sat heavy in his gut.

It had been that way when Asterion had married his little ex-nun and Poseidon had forced himself to attend the wedding, as he was supposed to. But he'd left the next day, escaping to New York and the endless round of business and parties that he'd thrown himself into.

Ridiculous to be so full of dread when the only thing waiting for him was Dimitra and her gimlet eye, and Asterion's blissful state of holy matrimony. Oh, yes, and a wedding, of course.

As the jet taxied towards the terminal Poseidon glanced at Andromeda, sitting opposite him. She was currently peering out of the window with wide eyes. On her hand glittered the massive sapphire he'd given her after a very public proposal while in Milan.

That had been the culmination of the perfectly orchestrated media campaign that he'd planned following the party in Monaco, consisting of a few other charity events in various European cities, a couple of 'private' dinners, and one midnight stroll along the Seine in Paris.

The media were in raptures over his courtship of a 'previously unknown redhead' and how romantic it was. And Dimitra had been grudgingly pleased with him—which was just as well because, when he'd thought Andromeda might kill him, he hadn't been far off.

That night in Monaco, after he'd dealt with scum in the shape of Simon Winchester, had proved to him that even a second night wouldn't be enough. That he had to have more. She'd agreed the moment he suggested it, and in the end she'd spent more nights in his penthouse than she had on his arm at the various events he'd taken her to.

By now he should be well-satisfied. But he wasn't.

It was as if the more he had of her, the more he wanted—which hadn't been his intent at all. His hunger for her was supposed to get easier to deal with, not more intense, and he was at a loss to explain why.

Every time he touched her he went up in flames, and he couldn't stop it. Really, the sooner they got this marriage over and done with and went their separate ways the better.

Andromeda straightened in her seat and glanced at him, her eyes shining. 'This place is beautiful, Poseidon. I had no idea.'

'There's a reason all the tourists flock here,' he said casually, shifting in his seat as the plane came to a halt.

Her gaze sharpened. 'You're very tense. Why?'

She was like this, he'd learned. Perceptive, picking up on his moods with almost insulting ease and asking him direct questions he'd rather not answer. She wouldn't ask her questions while they were in bed—they never talked there, too caught up in mutual pleasure—but when they were out of it, it was an entirely different matter. She ignored his idle flirting and insisted on serious conversation, which he didn't want to have. It was aggravating.

'Pre-wedding jitters,' he said, dismissive. 'I have a nervous temperament.'

'No, you don't.' Her red brows drew together. 'Are you worried about Dimitra?'

'I'm always worried about Dimitra.' He pushed himself up from the seat, unable to stay in it a second longer. 'Come, little siren. Time to disembark.'

She didn't say anything more, but the look she gave him told him that she wasn't letting it go.

He'd be fine. By tonight, the dread would be gone— he'd make certain of it. And if it hadn't, then he'd take Andromeda to bed and get rid of it that way.

The weather was beautiful, the air warm, and the drive from the airport to his residence, along the cliffs near Asterion's architecturally designed wonder of a house, was a pretty, winding journey.

He busied himself with phone calls to various people to see how the wedding arrangements were progressing, while Andromeda stared out of the window at the stunning beauty of the blue-green Mediterranean washing itself against the cliffs below.

His home was a more traditional affair than Asterion's, in whitewashed stone and red tile, with terraces stepped down the sides of the cliff, as well as a swimming pool. He also had an olive grove and grapevines, and staff that took care of both as well as the house while he was away.

Which was all the time.

The place held no memories. He'd bought it after Michel. Yet that cold, hard lump of dread sat heavier inside him as the car drew up to the house and his staff came out to greet him.

Settling in took a certain amount of time, as did receiving the various complaints and problems that had come up over the course of his absence. He took shameless advantage, sending one of his staff members to show Andromeda around. It wouldn't matter to her if he didn't do it himself, and besides, he *did* have a lot to do to get the wedding arranged.

Dimitra had wanted a vast affair, with many guests, as befitted a member of the Teras family, but since that would have involved more time than he wanted to spend, Poseidon had argued for a quick wedding, and the sooner the better. Dimitra had grudgingly agreed, muttering something about him having wedding night urgency. He hadn't argued. His grandmother didn't need to know that his fiancée had been spending every night in his bed already.

Later that evening, when there were no more urgent tasks he could reasonably use to distract himself with, Poseidon stepped out of the house and strolled over the white terrace to the pool, where Andromeda lay floating on her back with her eyes closed.

The sun was going down, painting her in tones of pink and gold, and her hair a swirling mass around her head. All she needed was more body paint and a tail and she would indeed be the mermaid he'd seen when he'd first met her.

Instead all she had on was a tiny green bikini. All he could think about was diving into the water and tearing it off her before carrying her over to one of the sun loungers and burying himself inside her.

Maybe that was exactly what he'd do.

'You're avoiding me,' Andromeda said as he began to take off his clothes. 'You've spent all day doing lots of things, and I bet they're all very important, but you're still avoiding me.'

A small shock went through him. Had it really been that obvious?

'Why on earth would I be avoiding you?' He began to undo the buttons of his shirt. 'Especially when all I've been able to think about all day is ravishing you on one of these sun loungers.'

'You're tense about something, and I know you don't want me to ask about it.'

He discarded his shirt and then his shoes, trousers and underwear. And then, finally, naked, he dived into the pool, relishing the cold shock of the water. Andromeda was still floating on her back, so he swam over to her.

'I can think of many better things to do than talk,' he murmured, tugging her into his arms.

She didn't protest, only slid her arms around his neck and leaned into him. Her skin was hot on his, in delicious contrast to the cool of the water, but her gaze was sharp as knives.

'You're very casual and dismissive when you don't want to talk about something,' she said. 'You turn it into a joke. And now you're trying to distract me with sex. Why is that?'

'Perhaps because I like jokes?' He slid one hand up her back and pulled at the tie of her bikini top, undoing it. 'And sex is more pleasurable than talking.'

'Ah, yes,' she murmured, letting him pull away her top so her breasts were free. 'Life is one big joke, isn't it? That's what you said.'

He had, that day of the gala at the Museum of Natural History, in the limo. When he'd also nearly told her about Michel.

'But,' she went on, pressing her bare breasts against his chest, so the softness of them made all the blood in his body rush south, 'I don't think that's true, is it?'

He didn't like the direct look in her eyes. He didn't like it at all. 'Not everything is a joke,' he said. 'Your naked body, for example, is—'

'Poseidon…' Her voice was very quiet, her gaze very steady.

All his muscles tensed—he could feel them—and it didn't seem to matter how hard he tried to relax, he couldn't get rid of the tightness.

'Why do you want to know?'

'Because you don't want to tell me—why else?'

Her warmth and her softness were too much…too distracting. If he wasn't careful he might let something slip, and he didn't want to. Michel and everything associated with him were in the past, and there was no reason to revisit it.

He let her go, leaving her floating, her glorious hair like kelp, the lights from the villa shining on her satiny wet skin.

'This isn't real, Andromeda,' he said, his voice hard, so that she would know this was crossing a line. 'This relationship of ours isn't an actual relationship. We're not together except in bed. And I don't have to tell you a damn thing.'

She only stared at him in the way he was starting to hate, as if she could see past all his walls, all his defences. As if she could see the idiot boy he'd once been, who'd let himself be broken for absolutely no reason at all.

'What are you so afraid of?' she asked.

The tension inside him got worse. He should leave. He should swim to the side, get out, get dressed, and go inside. Go to his gym and work himself into physical exhaustion. Because that would get rid of it. It always did.

Yet he stayed where he was. 'I'm afraid of nothing,' he said flatly, but they both heard the hollow note in his voice.

'Do you have anyone to confide in, Poseidon Teras?'

The look in her eyes had turned soft, which made him even more tense.

'Do you have anyone to talk to? Anyone at all?'

He didn't know why he was still in the pool, why he was still there when he should deal with this in his gym.

'I have my brother. What has that got to do with anything?'

'Everyone needs someone to talk to. Someone they trust. And you can trust me. I won't tell anyone.'

'Why?' he demanded. 'Why should I talk to you? Why does it even matter?'

She was silent for a moment, then she said, 'I knew Chrissy was unhappy at the end, no matter how much she kept insisting she was fine, but she refused to discuss it. And I couldn't talk to Mum, because she didn't want to hear that Chrissy was unhappy. God, I'd have given my eye teeth for someone to talk to…someone who'd listen.'

She paused, her gaze full of something that made his chest ache suddenly.

'Every life matters, Poseidon. Including yours.'

He wanted to deny it. He wanted to tell her that his life was no more important than anyone else's, and that also he wasn't her sister.

Her sister, who had been taken advantage of by an older man.

It wasn't the same. It *wasn't*.

In which case what does it matter if she knows? Who are you trying to protect?

Surely not himself. He didn't need to protect himself from anyone, because he wasn't vulnerable. Not any more. So why shouldn't he tell her? After all, it wasn't a big deal. It never had been.

'It's nothing,' he said, trying to sound casual. 'But if I tell you, I want you on that sun lounger.'

Because he might as well get something good out of this nonsense.

'I want you naked and I want you screaming my name.'

She stared at him for a moment, and then she reached down into the water. When she lifted her hands, she was holding her bikini bottoms in them. She tossed them negligently onto the side of the pool, then stood in the water with her arms folded, waiting.

'It was a long time ago,' he said. 'I barely remember. I think I was twenty. A close friend of my father's had become my mentor. He helped me deal with Hydra Shipping when I took it over, gave me support and advice, and I… I valued it greatly.'

It shouldn't have been so hard to say the words, yet he found he had to force them out.

'He was like a father to me, but he didn't see me as a son. He wanted…more.'

Andromeda's expression betrayed nothing, which was good, because the last thing he wanted was her sympathy.

'He told me he'd cut off all contact with me if I didn't give him what he wanted,' he went on, keeping everything very light and casual. 'So I did. Because I needed him. And afterwards he cut off all contact with me anyway.' He made himself smile. 'It was years ago, and I was very young and very stupid, and I let it matter. It doesn't now.'

A ripple of emotion passed over her face, though what it was he didn't know.

'If it doesn't matter then why are you so tense?' she asked.

But he'd had enough. He moved over to where she stood and pulled her into his arms, easing her naked body against his.

'I'm tense because you're naked and I want you.'

Her hands rested on his chest, not pushing, but definitely holding him at bay. She looked up at him. 'I think I can guess what he wanted from you. But…did *you* want it? Did you want him?'

A narrow flame of anger lit inside him—hot, burning. He'd never thought about that…never let himself think about it. Michel had been warm and kind at first, his fatherly approval balm to Poseidon's grief-stricken soul. And Michel had been proud of him, encouraging him to extend Hydra's operations and supportive of his ideas. He'd often told Poseidon that he was the son he had never had, and Poseidon had loved him like a father.

So when the suggestions had come—that Poseidon could perhaps give back the love Michel had given him—Poseidon hadn't understood. Not at first. Then, when he had, he'd tried to be kind, refusing Michel gently. He hadn't been inclined that way sexually, and had never expected the man he'd thought of as a father to see him as anything more than a son.

But then Michel had become insistent. Poseidon was beautiful, he'd said, so was it any wonder that he wanted him? Just once, he'd promised. That was all it would be.

Poseidon had tried to be firm, but then Michel had wept and pleaded, telling him that he loved him, that surely Poseidon could give him just one night. That wasn't much in return for everything Michel had given him. And Poseidon, who'd always felt too deeply and cared too much, hadn't wanted to hurt him.

Nothing would change between them, Michel had promised. *'Indulge an old man,'* he'd said. *'It's only sex...no big deal.'*

You didn't want it.

No, he hadn't.

But he'd given Michel what he'd wanted, and he'd told himself that it *wasn't* a big deal, and had forced himself to believe it. Afterwards he'd expected their relationship to go back to what it had been, just the way Michel had told him it would.

But it hadn't. Because Michel had never spoken to him again.

'What does it matter if I wanted it or not?' Poseidon snapped, the steady anger burning inside him even though it shouldn't. Even though it had been years. 'It made no difference in the end.'

A flame leaped in her eyes, fierce and hot. 'It *does* matter. If you didn't want it then it was sexual assault, Poseidon. It was rape. No matter if you said yes. You didn't want it. He assaulted you.'

The words felt too sharp, like knives cutting away parts of him. How could it be assault? He'd agreed to it and he hadn't fought it. Michel hadn't hurt him. He hadn't enjoyed it—even if he had been that way inclined, he wouldn't have enjoyed it, because he simply hadn't ever seen Michel in that light—but his enjoyment or otherwise hadn't mattered.

So you didn't feel dirty afterwards? You didn't feel used? You told yourself you were fine, that it wasn't a big deal, but you lied. You've been lying to yourself for years.

He ignored the thought. 'Don't.' He gripped her, hard. 'It's over. It's in the past. Leave it there.'

But of course she didn't.

'My sister was assaulted. Simon was older than she was and he showered her with gifts. He used her, manipulated her. He gave her drugs and then used her addiction to share her with his friends. She didn't say no to him. She loved him. But I know she didn't want what he did to her either.'

'I'm not your sister,' he said roughly. 'It was different.'

'How? He was older than you. A powerful businessman. He manipulated you in the same way Simon manipulated Chrissy.'

There was something cold inside him that his anger hadn't melted and probably never would. A shard of ice that he'd ignored, telling himself it wasn't there. The ice that had settled inside him the morning after he'd got home from Michel's, when he'd got into the shower and had stayed there an entire hour, scrubbing and scrubbing. He didn't know what exactly he'd been trying to wash off. All he knew was that no amount of scrubbing had made him feel clean.

And then, when he'd called Michel the day after that, assuming their relationship would go back to the way it had been, the call had gone straight to voicemail. Michel had never called him back. Never emailed him, never texted. And when Poseidon had visited him he hadn't answered the door.

He'd cut him off cold and Poseidon had never known why.

You do *know why. He never wanted you. Only your body.*

It was a mistake he would never make again.

'I think this conversation is at an end,' he said, gripping her harder. 'Time to give me what you promised, little siren.'

His grip was punishing, the glittering blue of his eyes hard and sharp as sapphires. Everything about him was hard, and Andie hadn't fully comprehended that until now. His body, obviously, and his sex, long and hot, pressing against her stomach. But there was a hardness in his smile, in his laugh, in his voice, when he made everything sound casual and unimportant.

He'd armoured himself—she could see that now. He'd armoured himself with his looks and that smile, that laugh, hiding his true nature away. But she suspected she knew what his true nature was. She saw it whenever he took her in his arms, when he burned like a flame with passion and intensity.

And now she understood why he needed his armour.

He'd been taken advantage of. He'd been groomed.

He'd been manipulated and used, his trust betrayed, and it was obvious that he blamed himself.

Stupid, he'd told her. He'd been stupid.

Yet he wasn't to blame, and now she was burning with helpless fury. Not at him, but at the man who'd hurt him.

'Is he dead?' she demanded. 'The man who hurt you? Or is he still alive? Tell me where he lives. I'll call the police.'

A muscle jumped in Poseidon's jaw. 'Andromeda—'

'He hurt you. I can't let that stand—I can't.'

Rage burned through her like wildfire. This was what Chrissy had had happen to her. A powerful, older man manipulating someone younger, more naive, using their own desires against them.

'You didn't deserve the hurt he caused and he deserves to pay.'

Poseidon shook his head. 'He's dead. He doesn't matter any more.'

But he did matter. She could see it in the tension in Poseidon's shoulders, in the tightness in his jaw, in the hard glitter of his eyes.

She'd seen it the moment the plane had landed. Because when she'd looked at him sitting opposite her, his gaze fixed out of the window of the jet, every line in his beautiful face drawn tight, she'd realised, with a kind of shock, that he'd come to matter to her.

It had happened slowly, over the weeks after that night in Monaco, as she'd attended events with him and spent nights in his arms, and she wasn't even sure how. They hadn't talked about anything meaningful or serious, only about movies and books, or occasionally a rousing argument about politics. After which he'd take her to bed, and there was definitely no talking then.

Still, she'd come to learn more about him than she'd intended. He was incisive and perceptive when it came to political arguments, and also well-read. He had an interest in technology, which didn't surprise her, and in philosophy, which did. He thought deeply about things, and he was far more considerate than she'd ever have guessed, and it had come as a shock to find that she liked him.

It had come as a shock to find that his feelings mattered to her, too. That she didn't like him being tense because it meant something was bothering him, and she wanted to know what it was so she could help.

She'd never expected the reason for his tension to be the fact that he'd been assaulted by an older man—and it *had* been an assault. Poseidon didn't want to accept that, it was clear, but that was what it had been. Why else would there still be so much anger in his eyes? He'd told her it didn't matter now, that it was in the past. And, sure, it *was* in the past. But it certainly still mattered. Because it was obviously still hurting him.

His hands were nearly painful, digging into the soft flesh of her hips, but she didn't tell him to let her go. She was so angry for him, and she wanted to do something, but she didn't know what. He didn't want to talk about it, and she knew she couldn't push him—that wouldn't be right. Nor would putting her own anger onto him.

She hated not being able to do anything. *Hated* it.

She hadn't known what to do with Chrissy either. All she'd been able to do was be there on the end of the phone, listening to Chrissy as she told Andie about the latest party she'd attended, hearing the hollow sound of her sister's voice. There had been despair in it too, but Chrissy hadn't wanted to talk about what was wrong, and Andie hadn't pushed. She'd been forced to stand silently by as Chrissy slipped further and further away.

Tears of frustration pricked at her eyes, but she knew he wouldn't want her crying over him either, so she blinked them fiercely away. 'Tell me what you need,' she said. 'Anything at all. I'll give it to you.'

He didn't say a word, only bent his head and took her mouth. She let him in. He was so hot, and she could taste the desperation in his kiss. He was running from it, she suspected. Trying to put what had happened with his mentor behind him—to minimise it, pretend it didn't exist. But she knew how the past wouldn't stay where you put it. How it kept creeping in, no matter how hard you tried to push it away.

She'd embraced hers in the end, since her sister seemed so set on haunting her, and had turned her life into a crusade. Yet she could understand why he didn't want to do the same. He'd trusted the man who'd used him…who'd manipulated him. Who'd made him do something he hadn't wanted to do. No wonder he didn't want to come back to this island. What memories must there be here for him?

His mouth became hotter, more demanding, and then abruptly he broke away, pulling her over to the edge of the pool. He got out, then tugged her after him, carrying her, still wet, over to a sun lounger and laying her on it. Then he followed her down, his hot, slick skin sliding over hers, his weight pinning her to the cushions. She reached up and ran her hands over his powerful muscled shoulders and down his strong back, glorying in the feel of his skin.

'I'm sorry,' she said, meeting his gaze. 'I shouldn't have pushed you into telling me. I just…wanted to help you if I could.'

'You can't help everyone, Andromeda. Some people don't need it.'

'You don't?'

'No.' His gaze had darkened, and it was sharp as it looked into hers. 'And I don't need saving.'

It felt as if he'd ripped some kind of protective layer off her. 'I'm not trying to—'

'Aren't you?' Gently he took her hands from where they rested on him and put them down on either side of her head. He held them there. 'Isn't that what you're doing with your cause? With your addiction service? You're trying to make up for the fact that you didn't save her.'

She took a breath, feeling almost winded. 'You think I don't know that? That I don't think about that failure every day?'

'You didn't fail, Andromeda. I told you that.' His gaze was merciless. 'And I'm not a new cause for you to champion, understand? We're sleeping together, and in a couple of days you'll be my wife, but that's where our story ends.'

They hadn't talked about how long they would continue sleeping together, and they hadn't talked about what would happen after the wedding. She'd assumed that they'd go their separate ways, since that was what their agreement had been about, and she'd thought she'd be fine with it.

But hearing him say it so bluntly made her feel… bruised.

He's got under your skin and you weren't supposed to let him.

She shoved the thought aside. She was fine—she wasn't hurt. She knew this wasn't supposed to go on longer than the wedding, that it was just sex and nothing more, so why the thought of it ending should be painful, she had no idea.

'You're *not* a cause,' she said. 'I was only asking if you were okay.'

There was anger in his eyes—she could see it glittering there. This thing with his mentor was an unhealed wound and she'd jolted it. Now he was lashing out.

The realisation made her own anger drain away.

This wasn't about her. This was about what had happened to him, and the fact that no matter how many times he said it didn't matter, it still did.

Like Chrissy did.

'Look,' she said in a quieter tone. 'I know you're not a cause, and I'm not trying to turn you into one. I only wanted to help.'

He said nothing for a long moment, just staring at her, and she couldn't tell what was in his eyes now.

'I meant what I said,' he murmured. 'This *will* end, Andromeda. I don't do relationships—not with anyone.'

Had she given herself away somehow? Made him think that she'd been hurt when he'd told her that? Because she wasn't. Not at all. In fact, that was what she meant to say.

But what came out was, 'Why not? Is it because of what happened with *him*?'

He smiled, but it was hard and brittle. She could see that now. Practised.

'No, why would it be? Michel did teach me one lesson, though. Caring about anything is a mistake. Wanting anything too deeply is a mistake. Feelings in general are a mistake. And they're not a mistake I'm willing to make again.'

She should have left it there, but she couldn't stop herself from asking, 'Why are feelings a mistake? I thought you didn't want him.'

'I didn't. What I wanted was my father back. Now, this conversation is definitely over.'

She could see that he meant it and knew she'd have to let it go. But her heart ached for some mysterious reason known only to itself.

It seemed too bleak not to care. Bleak and lonely. Also, you *had* to care at some point, didn't you? How else could things change? How else could you save people?

Yet it wasn't the time to debate that now. They weren't

going to be together much longer anyway, and she didn't want to waste any more moments with him arguing.

All she could do was reach up and pull his head down, taking his mouth, kissing him deeply, passionately, letting him know that while they weren't in a relationship she still wanted him, and he could do with that what he wanted.

And what he wanted appeared to be escape. So she let him spread her thighs, and when he thrust inside her she lifted her hips to meet his. Then she wound her legs around his waist, giving herself up to him and to the pleasure that he was giving her.

He took her hard, driving himself deep into her body, his mouth on hers, ravaging. He bit her lower lip and then nuzzled down her throat, licking her skin, biting the sensitive cords at the side of her neck. There was a desperation to him, a rawness that he only ever let out when she was in his arms, and she took it, letting her hands caress the strong muscles of his back.

When he put a hand down between her thighs, to touch and caress her there, making her gasp and arch against him, her gaze took in the storms in his deep blue eyes and she knew she was losing something.

She wasn't sure what it was, but it scared her. And when the orgasm came for her, barrelling over her like a freight train and causing the world to explode into flame, she had a horrible feeling that what she was losing was her heart.

CHAPTER NINE

ANDROMEDA STOOD IN the living area of the villa, her glorious figure swathed in the simple gown of white silk that was to be her wedding dress.

Poseidon had made it clear that he wanted to choose the gown himself, though obviously she'd have to like it too, and she'd let him. He didn't ask himself why that was important—just as he didn't ask himself why an unfamiliar possessiveness crept through him whenever he looked at her.

He didn't ask himself why he couldn't settle to anything, either, when surely, after telling Andromeda about Michel the night before, he should feel calmer. Yet he didn't.

Both her questions and her fury had bothered him, making him feel as if she'd ripped a bandage off a wound he hadn't realised was only half-healed, and no amount of putting that bandage back on would help.

He didn't want to think about the night he'd spent with Michel and he never thought about the morning after. Never thought about the days following, when he'd tried to get in touch with him, to resume their friendship, hoping it would go on as if nothing had happened, the way Michel had promised him.

Only to get back silence.

He'd never told anyone what had happened with Michel—not Dimitra, not Asterion—because it didn't concern them. And not because he felt shame or worthlessness. Yes, he'd made a mistake in giving Michel what he'd asked for, but that was all it had been. An error of judgement. It really wasn't worth getting so furious about.

You know it wasn't just an error of judgement.

That cold feeling crawled through him again, but he ignored it. He was good at ignoring it. He'd spend fifteen years doing so, after all. The main thing was that now he'd told her she'd stop asking questions and leave the past to lie where it was.

He didn't want their last few days together marred by more arguments over something that had happened a long time ago.

Only a few more days and yet you're dressing her up in a wedding gown of your choosing and wanting to get all the details right.

But he was tired of listening to his thoughts, so he ignored that one too and stared at her instead.

'Hmm,' she said, studying herself in the full-length mirror, fiddling with a fold of fabric at her hip. 'Do you think this needs adjusting?'

It didn't. Nothing needed adjusting. The dress was perfect, as he had known it would be, the silk wrapping around her curves, the strapless style cupping her luscious breasts. The frothing skirts had been sewn with crystals, making it look as if she'd been dipped in diamonds, and there were more crystals sewn into the bodice. She glittered and, with her red-gold hair loose, she looked like a goddess.

His goddess.

She's not yours, though. Remember?

Everything in him tightened, as if with denial—which was pointless. Because of course she wasn't his and never would be. Perhaps he'd claim a wedding night, but after that they would be going their separate ways.

He strolled over to where Andromeda stood and gave her an outrageously appreciative look in the mirror. 'It's perfect,' he said. 'Change nothing.'

Colour rose in her cheeks, but her gaze when it met his in the mirror was challenging. 'You shouldn't be seeing me in my gown before the big day.'

'If it was a real wedding then, no, I shouldn't.' He circled her, running his eyes over her just to be sure everything was perfect. 'But since it's not a real wedding it doesn't matter.'

'And what happens after the wedding? We haven't talked about it.'

He came to a stop behind her and shrugged. 'We'll have our honeymoon and then we'll go our separate ways.' He lifted his hands and put them on her silk-clad hips. He really couldn't get enough of touching her. 'If you don't want to continue sleeping together for our honeymoon, that's fine. But you should know that I have plans for a wedding night.'

'Oh?' she murmured. 'You have, have you? Well, you might get one. If I decide to give you one.'

A strange jolt of electricity went through him, as if a part of him wasn't happy at the thought of her refusal. Strange… He'd admit to feeling a little possessive of her in that gown, but when it came to sex it shouldn't matter to him if she refused him. It wasn't as if he hadn't had her before, many times over.

He turned his head, brushed his mouth over the side of her neck, making her shiver. 'Are you really going to say no to me? *Can* you say no to me?'

She leaned back against him, relaxing into his body, and sighed. 'You know very well that I can't, Poseidon Teras.'

Satisfaction closed like a fist inside him and he wanted to growl with the pleasure of it. 'Good. I'll have you know I'm going to take shameless advantage of that.'

He brushed another kiss over the side of her neck, then lifted his head to find her gaze meeting his in the mirror once again.

There was something open in it…a vulnerability that stole his breath away.

'Chrissy was always the special one,' she said. 'She had the beauty and she was smart. She got fantastic marks at school. She was supposed to go to university, be successful. While I… I worked hard, but I wasn't a straight-A student like she was. I wasn't as good with people, and I wasn't as beautiful. She said I was jealous, like I told you, but… I guess I wanted what she had.

I wanted the beautiful man and the expensive gifts. I wanted to be special.'

She glanced at herself in the mirror, at the crystals sparkling along the bodice of her gown, glittering like stars, then at him again.

'And I feel special, Poseidon. *You* made me feel special.'

He found himself rooted to the spot, as if she'd struck him with a lightning bolt, searing him all the way through. Women told him that they wanted him all the time, told him that they loved the pleasure he gave them, but no one had ever told him that he made them feel special.

'It's just a couple of gowns,' he said, his voice unaccountably rough. 'And a few parties. It's nothing.'

'No,' she said. 'No, I'm not talking about the gowns. I'm not talking about the parties, either. I'm not even talking about the sex—though that's part of it.' She turned around suddenly and looked up at him. 'It's you. You listen to me. Oh, you make it seem as if you don't, with your smiles and your jokes and your casual asides. But you listen. You know what's important to me. Any man could have offered me money in return for being his bride, but you offered me more than that. Ongoing sponsorship. Publicity. Exposure. You introduced me to people who could help. And you planned a special event just for me and Chrissy's Hope because you knew it was important to me.'

The intensity in her eyes made him uncomfortable. Made him want to deny it. Because it had been nothing.

A few words in the right ears and money he wouldn't ever use himself.

'I was being a businessman. It wasn't for you, Andromeda. It was all for me, and for Dimitra.'

'Perhaps. But, like I said, another man would have offered me just the money, or maybe even threatened me. They wouldn't have kicked Simon out of that casino, and they certainly wouldn't have sat down and held my hand and listened as I spilled my guts about Chrissy.'

He remembered that night in Monaco and the feel of her cold hands in his, the grief in her green eyes. A grief he'd wanted so badly to ease, not knowing how. The only thing he had thought to offer her was the comfort of his touch and hope that was enough.

'That was only because I wanted to get you into bed,' he said—because surely it had only been that. 'Nothing more.'

But she shook her head. 'You're wrong. You know, I was expecting you to be just like Simon, but you're not. Not in any way. You're more of a decent man than he is or ever will be.'

'You make me sound like a paragon.' He tried to smile. 'I don't like pedestals, little siren. I'm not suited to them.'

She didn't answer that, only giving him the most direct stare and making his breath catch. 'You do know it wasn't your fault, don't you?'

Another shock went through him, shaking him to his foundations. 'What?' His smile felt pasted on. 'I'm not sure what you're talking about.'

But he did know. They both did.

'You're a good person, Poseidon,' Andromeda said. 'It wasn't your fault.'

She stepped close to him and laid a hand against his cheek, then she went up on her toes and pressed a soft kiss against his mouth.

He found his hand was at the small of her back, bringing her even closer. But not only because he was hard for her—even though he was. He just couldn't bear the distance between them. He wanted her warmth and her scent, the sweetness of her physical presence.

She let him, and then laid her head on his chest—a gentle weight that somehow felt heavier than mountains. He wanted to wrap his arms around her. He wanted to hold her not for any other reason but the sheer joy and comfort of it.

He'd never wanted to hug anyone before, and he couldn't remember the last time anyone had hugged him. His mother had always been too interested in her tempestuous relationship with his father, and his father hadn't been a physically effusive man except with his wife. Asterion had clapped him on the shoulder in a brotherly way a couple of times, but that had been it.

So now, when Andromeda's arms slid around his waist, holding him, the weight in his chest, the heaviness of it, increased somehow. She was soft, and much smaller than he was, yet it felt as if she was the one anchoring him in place.

His resistance faded, his arms tightening around her,

and then they were standing there, holding one another, her head on his chest, his lips brushing her hair.

He closed his eyes, felt something shifting inside him and settling into place, like the final piece of a jigsaw puzzle. By telling him how special she'd made him feel she'd given him a little piece of herself. It was a gift. *She* was a gift. And he needed to give her something in return.

No, that was wrong. He didn't *need* to. He *wanted* to.

'I wanted Michel's approval,' he heard himself say roughly. 'I was desperate for it. My father had always favoured Asterion more than me, and nothing I did seemed to make any difference to him. But I didn't have to do anything for Michel. He was proud of me no matter what. At least…that's what I thought initially. I didn't know he'd always wanted more.'

His arms tightened fractionally, holding her even closer against him.

'I didn't want him, and I told him so. But he pointed out all the things he'd done for me…said that one night was the least I could give him in return. I didn't know what else to do.' He paused, inhaling her familiar scent. 'After he cut off all contact, I thought I'd done something wrong.'

'You weren't stupid,' she murmured against his chest. 'What you said yesterday about yourself? Yes, you were young, but you weren't stupid and you didn't do anything wrong. He manipulated you.'

Poseidon didn't like how vulnerable that made him feel. How powerless. Intellectually, he knew it was true, that Michel *had* manipulated him. But even now, all these years later, it felt difficult to accept emotionally.

'Perhaps he did,' he said. 'Michel told me he only wanted a night…that it wouldn't matter, that everything would go back to the way it always was afterwards. And I believed him. I forced myself to believe him. Yet I came home the next day and spent an hour in the shower trying to get myself clean.'

The stain still lingers, doesn't it?

And that hadn't been the worst part. Despite what Michel had done to him—despite the trust he'd violated—Poseidon had still loved him like a father and had wanted their relationship to go back to the way it had been before.

Love. It was nothing but betrayal.

Andromeda didn't say anything, only held him tight, and somehow that was exactly what he wanted. Someone to hold him and to listen.

'I never told anyone,' he went on, and the words were getting easier, the urge to get it off his chest growing. 'I never told Asterion or Dimitra. I kept telling myself that it wasn't worth mentioning, that it was just a minor mistake. No big deal. But I think there was a part of me that never quite believed it. And I think there was deeper reason I never told anyone.' He took a breath. 'I didn't say anything because I was…ashamed. I felt dirty. It wasn't supposed to be a big deal yet it was.'

There was blackness behind his lids, but that was fine. The blackness was safe.

'And when he cut off all contact with me I felt…used.

As if the rest of me wasn't worth anything. But even that wasn't the worst part. The worst part was that even after I gave him what he wanted, and he cut me off without a word, I still loved him.'

Andromeda turned her face into the hard wall of his chest and closed her eyes. She could hear the beat of his heart, faster than it had been before, betraying his agitation. He was warm, though, and he smelled so good, so familiar. Yet every one of those powerful muscles was drawn tight.

The crystals of her gown were pressing painfully into her, but she didn't want to move. His arms around her were tight, as if he couldn't bear to let her go, and she didn't want him to. She wanted to stand there all day, in the circle of his arms, and hold him right back. Because it felt as if her touch was something he needed.

She hadn't meant to tell him about her own jealousy, even though she'd told herself she wasn't jealous of her sister, only envious. How she'd always wanted to be the special one and never was. But she'd stood there in the gown Poseidon had bought for her—her wedding gown—and he'd looked at her with such blatant appreciation. A beautiful man, who'd treated her with so much gentleness and respect. A beautiful man who'd been hurt, and who was possibly afraid to admit it. She'd wanted to give him something.

She'd been going to tell him that she wanted to stop sleeping with him. She hadn't planned on giving him a reason, either, because she didn't want to tell him that if they kept on doing this she was in danger of falling for him and the thought filled her with dread. Mainly because he'd been so clear that a relationship was never going to be on the cards. Not that she was ready for a relationship anyway, but still…

But he'd kissed her neck, put his warm hands on her hips, and she'd known she couldn't tell him that she didn't want him, because that would have been a lie she couldn't bring herself to say. What she'd wanted was for him to feel as special as he'd made her feel, so she'd told him about his effect on her, even though it had felt as if she was baring a part of her soul and shouldn't be.

His eyes had flared then, as if what she'd said was a shock to him, and her heart had contracted in her chest—because did he not know how special he was? Did he genuinely not know?

Then his arms had come around her, almost hesitantly at first, then tighter, and he'd brought her close, and then he'd begun to speak, to tell her about Michel, and now she was crying. Pressing her face against his chest because she didn't want him to see her tears. He had enough to bear.

He was giving her something of himself too. Something he'd given to no one else—not even his brother.

You can't allow it to mean anything to you. You're already in deeper than you expected.

Oh, she knew that. But how could she allow what he'd said to mean nothing? This was something raw, painful, and deeply personal, and she'd heard the roughness in his voice. It had been hard for him to say, and yet he'd said it to her.

Of course it meant something, and to deny that would be wrong.

In that case, you have to be honest with yourself. You're in love with him.

Her heart was full and aching in her chest, a sweet agony. For him and what he'd gone through, and all alone.

It must have been a special kind of hurt too. Because even at twenty he would have been tall and powerful, no one's idea of a typical victim. But the force hadn't come from physical altercation. It had come, maybe even worse, from emotional manipulation. And he was a man of deep feelings, no matter how he insisted that he didn't care about anything.

It wasn't fair. It was wrong on just about every level.

And, yes, she loved him. She'd fallen for him a long time ago. Perhaps it had even been when he'd put his coat around her shoulders the day they'd met, in such a respectful and gentlemanly fashion, totally at odds with the man she'd thought he was.

But she knew now why he didn't want a relationship. Why he couldn't do love. Because love had been tainted for him by Michel. So perhaps it was best if she didn't tell him how she felt and kept that to herself.

It was going to make everything that much more painful, though.

More tears pricked her eyes, but she didn't let them fall. She wouldn't think about it, her stupid heart. He was the most important thing, not her feelings, and this moment was his, not hers.

'Nothing you did was wrong,' she said, her voice muffled by his shirt and his chest. 'And nothing you felt was wrong. He was the abuser. He manipulated your emotions and used them against you to get what he wanted. And love doesn't disappear instantly just because someone hurts you.'

She didn't look at him, because this was his private pain and she didn't want to force herself on him.

'Chrissy loved Simon right up until the end. Even though he hurt her and betrayed her.'

His arms still held her tightly and she felt his cheek press against the top of her head. Her heart ached. He was so much bigger than she was, so much stronger, and she felt almost enveloped by him. Yet he was holding her fast, as if he didn't want to let her go. As if he needed her.

For a long moment she stood there, listening to the beat of his heart, her eyes closed, breathing in his scent, loving his warmth. Then she felt his arms loosen around her and his body shifted. Only then did she look up at him, meeting his blue eyes, dark and depthless with an emotion she didn't recognise.

He didn't move away, only lifted his hands and cupped her face between them. 'And she hurt you, didn't she?' he asked gently.

The question was a shock. She wanted to deny it— tell him that it wasn't about her feelings. Because what did her feelings matter when Chrissy was gone? But the truth was that Chrissy hadn't listened, had ignored all her warnings, and if she hadn't things might have been different. And, yes, that hurt.

'She didn't listen to me,' Andie said. 'Mum didn't listen to me. Chrissy didn't want to believe that the path she was heading down was the wrong one, and Mum wouldn't hear a bad word said against her. I felt so helpless. So…useless.'

'You are neither,' he murmured, looking at her so intently she had no breath left. *'Asteri mou*, you're brave, and strong, and caring. You're special, Andromeda. You're the most special woman I have ever met.' He bent his head, brushing his mouth over hers. 'Let me show you how much.'

She didn't protest when his hands dropped to the zip on her gown, easing it down, then gently pulling away the fabric until eventually she was standing there only in her knickers.

Carefully, he draped the gown over the back of the couch, then came back to her, falling to his knees in front of her. He lifted his hands and ran them caressingly over her breasts, hips, and thighs, before leaning in and kissing her stomach. Then his hands moved to the waistband of her knickers and he pulled them down her legs, helping her step out of them before gripping her hips and kissing his way down between her thighs. He licked her, long and deep, his hands stroking and touching, mapping her curves with such reverence that the tears she was holding back stung once again.

He tasted her like wine, in slow sips that had her

thighs quivering and cries of ecstasy gathering in her throat. He explored her tenderly, taking his time, holding her as if she was the most precious thing in the universe.

He knelt there and worshipped her, and when she was shaking between his hands he rose to his feet, picked her up and carried her to the couch. Then he laid her on the cushions, stripped his own clothes off and followed her down.

Andie lifted her arms to him, welcoming him as he stretched out over her. the slide of his hot, bare skin over hers was an intimate pleasure she knew she'd never get tired of. And when he positioned himself, she reached down and guided him home.

He slid into her and it felt perfect. So right. So good. She lifted her legs and wrapped them around his waist, holding him deep inside her. He stared down at her as he began to move, and she could see the desire, the depth of his hunger for her. She gloried in it, spreading her hands on his powerful shoulders and stroking down his muscled back, touching him with the same care and reverence he was using to touch her. His deep blue gaze was her entire world.

This magic they created between them would end soon, but she didn't want it to. She didn't want to lose this—she didn't want to lose him. Yet it was going to happen, and there was nothing she could do about it. He didn't want a relationship—he was so clear about that—and she couldn't insist. It wasn't her place and it didn't feel right, not given what had happened to him.

You'll have to be happy with this, because this is all you'll ever have.

Her heart felt raw and bruised, and there was pain beneath the pleasure. But she ignored all of it and let herself sink into the ecstasy, let herself feel, for the first time, as if she really was as special as he told her she was.

As the orgasm overtook her she clung tightly to him, and when she fell, he fell with her. As the pleasure drowned them both, she knew one thing: she was going to have her beautiful man, and she was going to have her beautiful gown, and her beautiful wedding, in a beautiful church. She wouldn't be able to keep any of it, but she'd be grateful for it nevertheless.

After all, it was more than her sister had ever had.

CHAPTER TEN

THE LITTLE CHURCH was full as Poseidon waited by the altar. It was mostly full of friends of Dimitra's and other assorted island aristocracy, since she'd insisted on inviting as many people as she could.

Asterion stood next him as his best man, a silent, steady presence, currently gazing with adoration at his wife, Brita. The exquisite ex-nun was sitting with Dimitra and gazing back at Asterion with the same sickening adoration.

Though Poseidon barely noticed. A curious tension sat inside him that felt almost like dread, but surely couldn't be. He was marrying Andromeda, and it was going to make Dimitra happy and the shares of the family trust secure, so what on earth was there to dread? And after the wedding they'd have a wedding night, then a wonderful honeymoon, before going their separate ways. There was nothing at all to fear.

To distract himself, he thought again of yesterday, and the feel of Andromeda's body against his, the way she'd fitted in his arms, her arms tight around him. Holding him as if he mattered.

He hadn't felt as if he'd mattered for a very long time—he could admit that to himself now. Michel had made him feel worthless, and yet Andromeda's simple acceptance of what had happened to him, her insistence that he'd done nothing wrong, that his emotions around Michel hadn't been wrong either, had eased a tightness in him in a way he couldn't articulate.

It was still hard to admit to himself that what Michel had done to him *was* a big deal, that it *had* been assault. Essentially, he'd been groomed—which was very difficult to accept, because he wasn't a victim in any way, shape, or form.

It was still hard to accept that his love for Michel wasn't wrong either, considering how it had been used against him. She'd told him that none of it was his fault but, again, while he knew that intellectually, emotionally it was a different story.

Yet there was a certain freedom in accepting what she'd told him, and he hadn't realised that until she'd said the words. It was as if a weight had been lifted. Subconsciously he knew that a part of himself had always thought he was to blame for what had happened, and now it was as if she'd given him permission to leave the blame behind.

He'd felt lighter the night before than he'd ever felt in his entire life, and yet now, as he stared down towards the entrance to the church, ignoring the buzz of conversation from the assembled wedding guests, that weight was back and he wasn't sure why.

He was conscious of Dimitra's far too shrewd gaze

on him, as if she knew something he didn't—which didn't help.

She'd assisted Andromeda with her wedding preparations and had told him before the ceremony, with great certainty, that Andromeda was a fine choice because she'd never seen a woman so in love. Poseidon, she'd pronounced, had redeemed himself. The terrible Sea Monster was now tamed.

Yet right in this moment he didn't feel tamed. Something inside him was raging and he couldn't describe it. It was a strange not-dread, and a fierce anticipation, a raw possessiveness too, as if he would fight anyone who got in his way when it came to marrying Andromeda. Which was ridiculous—because who would stop him? She was going to walk down the aisle towards him soon, and then he'd take her off to his house for their wedding night and he'd keep her up till dawn. And after that their honeymoon in the Maldives, where he'd make love to her at every opportunity, wake up with her in the morning, talk to her about what interested her, what annoyed her, what made her passionate, her dreams, her hopes…

Then you will both walk away.

Yes. That was exactly it. That was the only reason all of that was even possible.

The church doors opened just then and in walked Andromeda. She was alone—she hadn't wanted anyone to give her away—and, in addition to the beautiful wedding gown she wore a silk veil that covered her face and extended down her back. She held in her hands some white peonies, with petals the same gossamer silk as her gown, and the first thing she did as she came into the church was look straight at him, her green eyes clear and steady.

A sudden rush of feeling gripped him hard by the throat. She knew his secret—the secret he hadn't even realised was a secret, the shame he hadn't been aware was shame. She knew and, despite knowing, she'd put her arms around his neck and kissed him, had let him into her body. She'd told him that he made her feel special, and in return she'd made him feel as if he wasn't that stupid boy he'd once been. The boy who'd believed the lies he'd been fed, who'd given away a part of his soul because he'd been so desperate for love.

She'd looked at him, seen all that shame and those feelings of worthlessness, and she'd accepted him despite all that. He hadn't been aware of how badly he'd needed that until now.

His chest ached as she came closer. He felt raw, undone, and violently possessive in a way he never had before.

You can't feel this. Not about her. Not about anyone.

It was true. He'd tried not to feel anything at all after Michel, because that was safer. He didn't want to be vulnerable to anyone—not again—and yet this beautiful, special woman had somehow found her way beneath defences he'd thought rock-solid. A mistake.

Perhaps going on a honeymoon with her was a bad idea. Perhaps wanting a wedding night was a bad idea. Perhaps right after the ceremony they should go their separate ways. Yet even as he thought this a part of him growled in silent rebellion, and he knew damn well he wasn't going to give up his wedding night or his honeymoon. It was selfish of him, and maybe a risk he couldn't afford, but he was going to have them. He was going to have as much of her as he could before it was time to say goodbye.

She walked slowly down the aisle to him and it was all he could do not to give in to the urge to meet her in the middle, toss her over his shoulder and carry her off, away from all these prying eyes. Take her somewhere private, where it was just the two of them, so he could sate his hunger for her over and over until this fierce, burning feeling was no more.

But he stayed where he was, because he wasn't an animal, standing rigidly beside the altar as she came to stand next to him and the ceremony began. When the priest joined their hands and said the prayers, the words echoed in his head, sounding like the truth instead of the lies they actually were. And when Asterion stood behind them and the exchange of wedding crowns was performed, he could hardly hear the priest through the thunder of his own heartbeat.

But then Andromeda glanced at him, her green eyes calm and direct through her veil, her wedding crown the perfect addition, and somehow the rush of blood through his veins steadied. And the platinum circle of his wedding ring felt abruptly like her arms around him the day before, anchoring him.

Then at last there was the trip around the altar three times, and finally it was time to kiss his new wife. Again he had to battle with himself not to ravage her mouth, lift her into his arms and carry her away. He would do that later. He could control himself. It was nothing. This feeling was nothing.

The way it was nothing with Michel?

No, this wasn't the same. This had nothing whatsoever to do with Michel.

His kiss was light, a mere brush of his lips on hers, as chaste as he could make it. Though when he lifted his head and found her looking up at him, with glittering sparks of heat and amusement in her eyes, he almost kissed her again, because she was so beautiful and he wanted her so badly.

There would be photos and register signings after the ceremony, and a reception to get through, but Poseidon decided then and there that the reception could be damned. He wanted to take his new wife back to his house, where they could be alone. Dimitra wouldn't mind. All she'd see was a couple in love who were desperate to be together.

Once the formalities were over, he grabbed Andromeda's hand and pulled her down the church steps to the wedding car. 'I don't want to wait until after the reception,' he murmured as he pulled open the door. 'I want my wedding night now.'

She went pink. 'Now? But everyone will know exactly what we're doing.'

'Good,' he said. 'I hope they do. It'll only add to the illusion.'

It's not an illusion, though, is it?

He ignored that thought too, pulling her into his arms as soon as the car door was shut behind them. She was warm and sweet, relaxing against him, her veil draped over his arm, her head against his shoulder, and he kissed her long and deep and hungry.

'You're my wife now, Andromeda,' he murmured against her mouth. 'And I need to claim you.'

'You've already claimed me.'

Her voice sounded husky, and when he raised his head and looked down at her there was something fierce and glittering in her eyes, an emotion he couldn't name. It made his own heart clench like a fist in his chest.

'You claimed me the day you came out of your building and put your coat around my shoulders.'

His throat tightened. The dread that had gripped him at the beginning of the ceremony was creeping up on him again and coiling in his heart. Because although he might tell himself all he liked that he didn't know what emotion burned in her eyes, he knew all the same. She felt something for him, didn't she?

'Little siren,' he said, his own voice as husky as hers, 'this will end, remember? We will have a magnificent wedding night, and a glorious honeymoon, but after that this affair of ours will be over.'

Her gaze flickered a moment, then steadied. 'Yes. I know. You told me.'

'I can't give you more.'

He didn't want to have to repeat himself, but that look in her eyes… She couldn't feel anything for him. That was only going to end in pain for her.

Her hand came up, her fingertips touching his cheek-bone lightly. 'I know you can't.' Her voice was clear and steady, and yet there was a note in it that made him ache. A note heavy with yearning and regret.

She wants more.

But he couldn't give her more. He *wouldn't* give her more. And if she already felt something for him, then it made their eventual parting even more inevitable.

Which means you should say goodbye to her now. She deserves someone to make her feel special for the rest of her life, not just tonight. Not just for the next two weeks.

Ice crawled through his veins. He was a selfish man—he'd always been a selfish man—and taking a wedding night, having a honeymoon, was all about feeding his own lust, his own hunger.

You're just like Michel in the end.

The ice solidified, hardening inside him. He *was* like Michel, like her sister's boyfriend Simon. Men who used the emotions of others against them in order to satisfy themselves. He'd done it from the very beginning—from the moment he'd come out of his office to see her chained to that statue, shouting into her megaphone. He'd used her love for her sister and her grief to make her do something she didn't want to do. Then he'd used their chemistry to satisfy his own desire for her.

It didn't matter that she'd agreed to it all. It didn't matter that she'd told him he'd treated her with respect, that he'd made her feel special. He'd still made her do something she never would have even considered and he knew what that felt like. How in the end it made you feel dirty and used and worthless.

He couldn't do the same thing to Andromeda. He'd rather die.

Carefully, even though every part of him was stiff with denial, he eased her from his lap.

Her eyes widened. 'What's wrong?'

An ache was settling inside him, making his chest tight, even though he tried to ignore it. He had to do this now and he had to do this quickly—it would be better for them both.

Poseidon met her gaze. 'I'm sorry, Andromeda. But I've changed my mind. I think it's best if we end this now. I'll take you home and you can gather your things. My jet will be available to take you back to London tonight.'

Andie had no idea what had happened. She'd been in his arms, relaxing against him, relishing his heat and strength. The next moment he'd put her out of his lap and told her he was sending her home.

What had she done wrong?

When she'd walked through the church doors and seen him waiting for her at the altar, it had felt like a dream come true. No, it *was* a dream come true. She'd been wearing a beautiful dress, in a beautiful church, and was marrying a beautiful man, and then they were going off on a wonderful honeymoon.

The spectre of leaving him waited in the distance,

but she hadn't been thinking about it. Their separate ways could wait. She wanted to enjoy what she had now.

Except then, in the car, in his arms, she'd watched as the heat in his eyes had dimmed, become dark, and he'd pushed her out of his lap. Told her there would be no wedding night, no honeymoon. That she would be leaving now.

He did understand that she'd accepted that their affair would end, didn't he? She knew he couldn't give her more. She wasn't asking for more, anyway, and she was fine with it.

You're not fine with it.

Well, no, but she wasn't going to push. She never would—not with him.

Her heart was beating fast and she wanted to reach for him, pull his arms back around her, but she kept them in her lap instead.

'Why?' she asked, trying not to sound demanding. 'I thought we were going to have a wedding night at least.'

'I thought so too.' The vivid blue of his eyes was darkening into black now, the lines of his face becoming rigid. 'But, like I said, I changed my mind.'

Her throat tightened, a stab of pain shooting through her. 'Is it me? Was it something…?'

'No,' he interrupted quickly. 'It's nothing you did— nothing at all. A wedding night was something I wanted, Andromeda. In fact, I demanded it. Just as I demanded this wedding. You didn't want to marry me—you didn't want to have anything to do with me. But I made you. And I used your grief for Chrissy to do it.'

She knew immediately what he meant, and everything inside her turned cold. 'Poseidon, you're not him,' she said very clearly. 'You're not.'

He gave her a cool look. 'Am I not? Michel used my feelings for him, my love for him, against me. He used it to manipulate me into giving him what he wanted. Aren't I just doing the same thing to you?'

'No.' She couldn't keep the fierce note from her voice. 'No, you're not. You gave me a choice. You never forced me into it. Yes, part of it was my feelings for Chrissy, but *I* decided whether to do it or not. And you didn't threaten me with anything if I said no.'

'I wouldn't have given you the money if you'd refused.'

'That's not manipulation, Poseidon. You were very clear the whole way through about what you were prepared to give me and what you wanted in return. Even in Monaco you were clear. You didn't spring anything on me that I wasn't expecting.'

He shook his head. 'Perhaps. But what I'm doing now is definitely manipulation. I want that wedding night, Andromeda. And I want that honeymoon too. But it's not fair of me to take it when you want more.' He paused a moment, his gaze searching. 'And you *do* want more, don't you, little siren?'

Her heart lurched at the gentleness in his voice and there were tears in her eyes. She didn't want to cry, though, so she blinked them fiercely back. 'Look, I know what you said about us going our separate ways afterwards, and I can handle—'

'Andie,' he said very softly, 'that's not what you really want.'

She wanted to get angry, deny it. Tell him that he couldn't speak for her, and ask him what did he know about what she wanted anyway? But she couldn't find her anger now—and besides, what would be the point? She couldn't hide what was in her heart. Not when she felt this strongly, this powerfully. She'd always striven for honesty.

'No,' she said in a husky voice. 'You're right. That's not what I really want.'

A muscle jumped in his jaw. 'I can't give—'

'I know you can't.' This time it was her turn to interrupt. 'And I'd never force you or manipulate you into it.' More tears prickled, and this time she didn't blink them away. 'But I… I can't lie. I do want more. Because the truth is that I've fallen in love with you, Poseidon Teras.'

His gaze had darkened almost into black, but he didn't say anything. So she went on, because she might as well.

'I always told myself that it was Chrissy who had the white wedding dreams, not me, but that was a lie too. A lie I told myself because I didn't want to admit that I'm more like my sister than I should be. I wanted a handsome man to sweep me off my feet. I wanted the white dress and a beautiful church. And I wanted to be someone's wife. To be loved.'

His black lashes fell, his features tightening as if she'd delivered a mortal blow, but she hadn't said everything that was in her heart yet, so she continued.

'I love you, Poseidon. But not because you need saving, or because I can heal you, or because you're a cause I'm giving my all to. I love you because you listen, and you're thoughtful. Because you're intelligent, and you disagree with me, and that makes me think. You surprise me, and you respect me, and you make me feel special. And no one has ever given me any of those things.'

'Andromeda—'

'No, I haven't finished.' She took a shaky breath, gazing at the pure lines of his profile. 'I'm selfish. I want to keep all of it. But… I don't want it if you don't.' The tears escaped, sliding down over her cheeks, but she made no move to brush them away, just as she didn't try to keep the hoarse note of pain from her voice. 'The last thing I would ever do is force you to give me something you don't want to give.'

His lashes lifted then, and he looked at her. The expression on his face tore at her. Intensity burned there, along with something longing, something yearning, and a regret that broke her heart.

'I'm sorry, my beautiful little siren,' he said, his voice as husky as hers. 'I wish I could give you what you want. But I made a promise to myself years ago that the only things I will ever let myself care about are my brother, my grandmother, and my company. I can't give anyone anything more.'

He lifted a hand to her cheek and gently brushed away her tears.

'You deserve to be with someone who'll make you feel as special as you really are. Who'll give you all the love you deserve for the rest of your life. You deserve to have someone who hasn't been broken like I have.'

Her heart was tearing itself in two, pain radiating through her entire body. She'd had no idea it would hurt this much.

'You're not broken, Poseidon. Don't allow Michel that power. You're an amazing man, and don't let anyone tell you any different.' She leaned into his hand, allowing herself this one last touch. 'But I understand. And I want you to know that if there's one person in this world who loves all of you, every part of you—even the part that you think is broken beyond repair—that person is me.'

A raw and anguished expression flickered in his eyes, and for a second she thought he might change his mind.

Everything in her went still.

But then his hand dropped from her cheek and his gaze shuttered. 'Find someone who feels that way about you, Andromeda. That's the very least of what you deserve.'

She couldn't find even the slightest spark of anger with which to argue. Not that she wanted to get angry with him. He'd made his choice and, since that choice had been taken from him once before, this time she had to let him make it. She couldn't—wouldn't—force him or guilt trip him into choosing differently.

It wasn't his fault that she wasn't enough to make him change his mind. She hadn't been enough for Chrissy, either.

But one thing was clear. For her own sanity she

needed to put as much distance between them as possible, as quickly as possible.

He was right. It was time for her to go home.

She looked down at her hands, twisted in her lap. The silk of her wedding dress was spotted darkly with tears.

'I don't want to go back to your house,' she said. 'Just take me to the airport. Please.'

CHAPTER ELEVEN

POSEIDON SAT IN the darkness of his living room, clutching the tumbler containing his third straight whisky while he stared at the wedding ring circling the third finger of his left hand.

It was his wedding night, but he'd been as good as his word. Andromeda had wanted to go straight to the airport so that was where he'd taken her. And now she'd left for London, flying away from him into the night, and that was as it should be. That was what he'd wanted.

Yet recalling her face, and the tears streaming down it, ripped something apart deep in his soul. There had been a peculiar agony in watching her go up the stairs into the jet, the skirts of her wedding gown clutched in her hand, and he hadn't expected that. He'd thought he'd be relieved, if anything, because he had what he'd wanted at last. Her name on a marriage certificate, someone legally his wife, Dimitra's challenge met.

But the feeling in his heart wasn't relief, but pain. As if she'd taken a piece of his soul with her when she left. He didn't understand why. She loved him, she'd said in the car, and that had made a part of him leap in wild hope, while another part had felt frozen from the inside out.

What was hopeful about love? Love made you feel dirty. Love made you feel used. Love was agony. Love was a vulnerability that could be used against you when you were least expecting it. Love was power—a weapon that could deliver a mortal blow—and he would never willingly put that kind of weapon in anyone's hands ever again.

Losing his parents had left him vulnerable, because he'd loved them. Michel had taken advantage of that love. Michel had used it for his own ends. And Poseidon couldn't make the same mistake a second time.

So he'd had to let her go. He couldn't give her the love she needed, the love she deserved, and keeping her for only a wedding night and a honeymoon, knowing that she loved him, would only be to visit the same kind of emotional torture on her that Michel had visited on him.

He couldn't do it. He wouldn't. She needed to be free to find someone better than he was. Someone who could love her for the amazing woman she was and who had more than just sex to offer her. God knew, that was all the value he had. Michel had taught him that.

He had nothing else to give anyone.

Poseidon sat there for a long time, waiting for the pain in his heart to go away, but it didn't. It felt like grief, which was odd, because no one had died.

Finally, he heard voices in the hallway—his housekeeper's and another, much deeper. Then, at last, a tall figure strolled into the room.

'Emulating me, brother?' Asterion said, coming over to where Poseidon sat before settling into the chair opposite. 'I have to say, brooding doesn't suit you.'

Poseidon's fingers tightened around his tumbler. One day he'd have to tell Asterion about Michel, but he couldn't face it now.

'What are you doing here?' he demanded gracelessly.

'Someone said they saw Andromeda boarding the jet. By herself. So I thought I'd come and see what the issue was.'

'The issue is that she's gone,' he said flatly. 'So I suppose that's that.'

'I suppose so,' Asterion observed. 'If by "that" you mean drinking yourself into a coma.'

'It's a party.' Poseidon lifted his tumbler and tried pasting on his usual smile, but it took so much effort that he stopped. 'Please join me.'

'Thank you, but no.' Asterion leaned back in the chair and stretched his long legs out. 'I don't do pity parties.'

Poseidon tried his usual laugh too, but it came out sounding hollow. 'It's not a pity party. What are you talking about?'

Asterion's blue gaze, so like his own, merely stared back. 'Of course it is. You're sitting here, brooding like Heathcliff, drinking yourself into a stupor because your wife has left you.'

Poseidon decided to give up pretending. 'She didn't leave me. I told her to go.'

Asterion looked at him with mild curiosity. 'Why on

earth did you do that? Any fool can see you're madly in love with her.'

A shock went through him like lightning, sharp and hard. 'I'm not in love with her,' he said, ignoring the way his heart was pressing painfully against his ribs and how the words felt like lies in his mouth.

'Of course you are,' Asterion said patiently, using his elder-brother voice, as he'd used to do when Poseidon was very young. 'I saw the way you looked at her the moment she entered the church. And I saw the way she looked at you too. Even Dimitra did. So, again, why on earth did you tell her to leave?'

His brother was wrong—just flat-out wrong. He didn't love her. He *couldn't* love her. Love was a choice and he'd decided it wasn't for him.

'One day I'll tell you.' He lifted his tumbler and took another sip of his whisky, the alcohol burning like fire inside him. 'But now, suffice to say, I decided it was better for her if she left.'

Asterion frowned. 'Better for her how?'

He took another swallow of whisky. 'Let's just say I wouldn't wish love on my worst enemy.'

'Thank you for intimating that I am even worse than your worst enemy.'

Poseidon stared at him, trying to ignore the pain in his heart. 'How do you bear it?' he asked abruptly. 'How *can* you bear it?'

'Love?' Asterion smiled, as if he was remembering something very pleasant indeed. 'I don't "bear" love. I take it. I embrace it. I cover myself with it. I have it and it is more precious to me than anything else in my entire life.' He leaned forward, elbows on his knees. 'Love is a good thing, my brother. Believe me, I know. Don't be afraid of it. We lost our parents so young, but don't let those scars stop you from taking a chance at happiness.' His gaze, always serious, became even more so. 'And you deserve happiness, Poseidon. So does she.'

His heart clenched tightly in his chest, the ache in it getting even worse. Love was a good thing? Love meant happiness? Perhaps for Asterion it meant those things, but that hadn't been his experience. And what was happiness anyway?

She loves you. She made you happy.

He stilled. She *did* love him—she'd told him so. And her love had never made him feel guilty or dirty or ashamed. It had never caused him pain. Those things were also true. Her love was grounding. It made him feel good. Made him feel as if he had value. And in her arms he'd tasted something more than mere physical pleasure...something deeper...something that had felt a lot like...happiness.

She would never do to you what Michel did.

The knowledge settled in him like a stone thrown into a lake, sinking straight to the bottom and lying there, heavy with truth.

She was nothing but honest, nothing but straight up. She could have used his desire for her against him and she hadn't. Not once. And at the end, in the car, with tears streaming down her face, she'd let him make a choice. He hadn't chosen her, and even though that had caused her pain she hadn't protested, hadn't argued. She'd only told him once again that she loved him and then had let him push her away.

It was never about her, though, was it? It was always about you.

Poseidon's throat tightened, his heart weighted and achingly heavy. Perhaps that was right. Perhaps it really *was* about him. About his fear…about how, after Michel had cut off contact with him, he'd felt worthless. If there was nothing about him that anyone would want, why did he think he had anything of any value to offer Andromeda?

'Don't allow him that power. You're an amazing man. Don't let anyone tell you any different.'

That was what she'd told him in the car and he hadn't believed her. Because if he was so amazing, why had that man forced himself on him and why had he lied to him?

You're still giving him power. You're still letting him take your choice from you. Because if he hadn't been in your past you wouldn't have let anything come between you and Andromeda.

Understanding burst through him, so powerful that he could hardly breathe let alone speak. Because it was true. If nothing had happened with Michel, he would have brought down heaven if it had meant he could be with his siren.

All these years later and he was still letting Michel make his choices for him. Still letting him have power. And that wasn't love—he could see that now. Love *wasn't* manipulation. It *wasn't* a weapon.

Love was Andromeda's arms holding him.

Love was the look in her green eyes as she'd walked down the aisle to meet him.

Love was the tears that streamed down her face as she'd told him she would never force him to do something he didn't want to.

Love was the reason she fought her battles, for her sister, and he knew that she'd fight them for him too.

And love was the raw, passionate feeling in his heart, the pain in his soul. The grief he'd felt watching her walk up the stairs to the jet and fly away from him.

He loved her.

He loved her so much it was sweet agony and glory all rolled into one. It was standing on the edge of a cliff and jumping off into the terrifying void, only to fly...

Asterion nodded, as if Poseidon had spoken every word of his thoughts aloud. 'I think you understand now, don't you?' he said comfortably.

Poseidon lifted his tumbler, drained it, then put it back on the table next to him with a firm click. 'Tell Dimitra I have to go to London to retrieve my wife,' he said. 'It appears we missed our honeymoon flight.'

Asterion smiled. 'And your plans for a quick divorce...?'

'Are on hold,' Poseidon said as he strode for the door. 'Indefinitely.'

There was some muck-up with the flight plan and the jet ended up being diverted to Paris, where they sat on the Tarmac for what seemed like hours. Not that Andie was taking any notice of time.

She'd held it together until after the jet had left the island kingdom, then she'd burst into tears, watching the little island get smaller and smaller through the window of the plane.

She felt raw, and hollow, and she knew she was going to have to pull herself together when she landed in London, but for now all she wanted was to cry. She missed Poseidon so badly it hurt.

They hadn't spoken a word the rest of the interminable journey to the airport and he hadn't touched her again. And then, once they got to the airport, she'd got out of the car and hadn't looked back. She hadn't been able to bear to.

Now it felt as if a part of herself had been ripped from her chest, and she wished so badly that she could get angry about it. But, again, all her anger seemed to have gone. The only thing she felt was grief for what might have been.

You'll recover. You'll move on. That's what you did after Chrissy died.

She had—it was true. But if there was one thing she knew it was that grief changed you. You were never the same person after it had got its claws in you, and she wasn't the same woman who'd landed on the island a few days earlier.

She'd fallen in love with a man she'd never thought she'd even like, let alone love, then had her heart broken by that same man. It hurt. It hurt so much. Yet she wouldn't change it. Poseidon Teras was a man worth loving and she had no regrets. She wasn't going to stop loving him either. She'd probably continue to love him until the day she died.

Soon the flight plan mix-up was solved and the jet climbed into the air again, on towards London.

Andromeda wiped her tears away as they came in to land and hoped she didn't look too wrecked. She'd have to call herself a taxi or get a ride via the app on her phone. Hopefully she wouldn't get a chatty driver.

Then the stewardess—who'd politely left her alone for the flight, just surreptitiously passing her tissues when she needed them—opened the door of the jet and Andie, still in her wedding gown, gathered the skirts up as she got to her feet.

She went to the jet's door and stepped out onto the metal stairs. In the dimming light of a dull London evening she could see a long black car pulled up on the Tarmac, and a man leaning back against it with his arms folded.

A tall man. A *very* tall, powerful-looking man. And he was still wearing a morning suit.

Her heart gave one heavy, painful beat.

Poseidon.

Shock pulsed through her and for a long moment she just stood there, the wind tugging at her wedding gown, staring at her husband. Who stared back.

Then he pushed himself away from the car and straightened.

She was too far away to see the expression on his

face clearly, so she began to walk down the stairs, and as she did so her absent anger suddenly burst into life inside her.

What on earth was he doing here? And how dared he? How dared he break her heart into pieces by telling her to leave, only then to turn up here at the airport to meet her? What did he want? Had he forgotten something, perhaps? To stomp on the pieces of that heart of hers that he'd broken?

She'd sworn she wasn't going to be angry, but this was a step too far.

She reached the Tarmac and strode across it towards him. His face was set in fierce lines, his blue eyes were burning like gas flames—every part of him the intense, passionate man she knew he was deep down.

'What the hell are you doing here?' she demanded.

But he didn't give her a chance to go on, because by then he'd taken a couple of steps towards her and, before she could say another word, he'd swept her up and into his arms, holding her there so tightly she couldn't escape.

'What the hell am I doing here?' he echoed, his gaze burning down into hers. 'I'm here to tell you that I love you, Andromeda Lane. And that I made a mistake. I should never have let you leave and, now that I have you, I'm never letting you go.'

And just like that all the fight went out of her, taking her anger along with it. She looked up at him, her heart aching, the warmth of his body seeping into her and stealing all her resistance.

'I thought that love wasn't something you could give,' she said huskily.

'I thought that too,' he said. 'But then Asterion came to give me a piece of brotherly advice. He didn't understand why I'd let you go when it was clear I was in love with you and you with me.'

Her throat closed. 'Did you tell him…?'

'No. I will one day, but not yet.' His arms tightened around her. 'He made me realise that the problem wasn't love, *asteri mou*. The problem was me. The problem—as you so astutely put it in the car after the wedding—was me still letting Michel make my choices for me, and all because I was afraid.'

She couldn't resist it. She lifted her hand to his beautiful face. 'Oh, Poseidon…'

'And I knew that. Because if Michel hadn't been in my past, there wouldn't have been anything in heaven or earth that would have stopped me from being with you.'

He turned her to the car that was parked there, the driver having already opened the door.

'So I decided that I had to stop letting him steal choice from me. I decided that there is only one man in the entire world who gets to love you, to make you feel special, to give you all the things you've always wanted. And that man is me, little siren.'

He smiled, and his smile was warm and brighter than the summer sun.

'I am devastated to report that from now on I must insist on being your husband for the rest of your life.'

Her heart felt full, a flower unfurling and blooming

inside the cage of her ribs, and there were tears in her eyes yet again.

'I don't get a choice?'

Poseidon lowered her into the car and then followed her inside, shutting them both in the warm interior. Then he pulled her straight back into his arms.

'Naturally. You always get a choice, my beautiful wife.'

'Good,' she murmured as he bent his head to kiss her. 'Because in this instance my choice will always be you.'

EPILOGUE

POSEIDON SAT WITH his brother in the shade of the olive grove, enjoying another of the magnificent summers that the island put on, and listening to the sound of various children creating havoc around them. There appeared to be lots of screaming going on—something about a toy that his daughter Leni wanted, which one of her cousins had stolen from her or some such.

Leni was always screaming. She was definitely her mother's daughter.

He smiled indulgently as her older brother, Nico, at ten much more contained and grown-up than his six-year-old sister, came to the rescue.

Definitely his son, that one.

His sister-in-law Brita was sitting cross-legged on the grass, showing the other children the basics of a bow and arrow—most of them were Asterion's, except for the twins, Poseidon's youngest, Christa and Carlo, who were watching with big green eyes.

Archery practice was apparently now mandatory for a Teras child.

Asterion was watching his wife with adoration, but

Poseidon didn't find it sickening any more. Mainly because his own little siren was curled up at his side, chatting with a by now very elderly Dimitra about how they were opening up a few new Chrissy's Hope services in the States and planning some for Australasia as well.

Andromeda's charity was doing brilliantly, as he'd known it would.

Just then Leni came over and flung herself, still weeping, into Poseidon's lap.

He closed his arms around her. 'Poor little one,' he murmured, stroking his daughter's red-gold hair. 'Papa has you.'

Asterion glanced at him then, and the brothers shared a smile. Because now they both had what they hadn't even realised they wanted. Contentment. Happiness. Joy.

And in the end Dimitra had been right. Her choice of wife for both of them had been the right choice—the *only* choice.

Though it wasn't marriage that had tamed the Monsters of the Mediterranean.

It was love.

* * * * *